THE YOUNGEST MOUNTAIN MAN

The Youngest Mountain Man

Copyright © 1998

Published by: J and D Publishing, Curtis, NE 69025

ISBN: 0-7392-0241-3

Library of Congress Catalog Card Number: 99-93914

Printed in the USA by

MORRIS PUBLISHING

3212 East Highway 30 * Kearney, NE 68847

1-800-650-7888

Welcome to my New Beginning stories.
This as you know is Volume Two, "The
Youngest Mountain Man." If for any reason
you haven't read Volume One, "Those
Magnetic Sandhills," I recommend you
get a copy and read it first. If that
is not possible or if it has been sometime
since you have read Volume One, you may
want to read the following synapsis to
help you understand this story better.
As I wrote it, I tried not to give away
any surprises so if you do eventually
read Volume One it will be more interesting.

                    Mick Scarlett

Volume One "Those Magnetic Sandhills"

     Joe Jorden, the main character,
finds himself stranded in a small sandhill
town in Nebraska. He has left
Philadelphia after another disagreement
with his domineering father Gus. Gus
runs an arms manufacturing plant and
he and Joe had never gotten along very
well. Out of money and stranded, Joe
goes to work for a cafe owner for board
and room. After that job is completed,
he takes a job on a ranch. He has many
interesting experiences being a city
boy. As World War Two is raging in
Europe, it isn't long and he is drafted
into the Army. He sees action in France
but realizes how much he misses the sandhills and the people he has met. Joe
has two sisters in Philadelphia. Ann,
his younger sister, is outgoing, loves
the outdoors, and horses. While Ellen
is a socialite and loves the high class
living her father provides.

     That is as much as I dare disclose
about Volume One without giving away

the whole story and ruining it for you should you read it later. With this short narrative you will at least understand who Ann and Joe are when they are mentioned in Volume Two.

I hope you enjoy, "The Youngest Mountain Man."

Mick Scarlett

DEDICATION

I am dedicating, THE YOUNGEST MOUNTAIN MAN, to my parents, Bill and Bessie Scarlett.

Mom and Dad were true sandhillers as Hank Evans would say. Dad was born in Missouri and moved to Boone County Nebraska as a boy. When he was sixteen, he ran one of the first power hay sweeps in the Beaver Valley and ended up on the Mel Dorn ranch northwest of Bartlett. He just never bothered to go home. From then on he was hooked on the sandhills.

Mom was born to a German family also in Boone County. Her dad was from a German colony in Russia. Grandpa Esau came to America on a cattle ship when he was six years old. Growing up Mom worked on ranches in Boone County and a cafe in Lincoln, Nebraska until she and my father married.

Their first home was on Wolf Brothers and Reich West Ranch northwest of Bartlett. Dad was foreman on the west ranch, which consisted of approximately twenty three thousand acres. My sister, Karen was born there.

After starting on their own in Boone County, where I was born, they bought a section of sandhills west of Bartlett. We moved to the sandhills in 1950 when I was three years old.

I truly enjoyed growing up in the sandhills. Now after raising three children of our own here, my wife Kathy and I truly appreciate the problems our parents faced. It is a challenge to try and shape the lives of children, even while not under the influence of mind altering drugs such as alcohol. A distraction such as that could only make it worse.

To Mom, Dad, and all parents that try their best to raise their families right I say thank you.

I am including a poem I wrote New Year's Eve twenty five years after Dad's departure. Following the poem is a picture of Mom and Dad taken in 1947, the year I was born.

Mick Scarlett

AN ODE TO DAD TWENTY-FIVE YEARS AFTER HIS DEATH

Twenty five years ago tonight,
In a bed so far away,
Tobacco and time snuffed out Dad's bright light,
Thus was the end of his life's foray,

He went off to join God's crew,
Off to see Ed, Ralph, Ed, and Mel,
Off to see what he could do,
Since then to be joined by Elmer, Walt, Pete, Wayne, and Mel,
To run God's ranch since earthly life was through,

I doubt if they get much work done,
With all the jokes and stories to tell,
I'm sure they have a lot of fun,
At times I bet God wants to tell them to go to hell,

Unknown to the crew,
Though younger than the rest,
They have been joined by Bow too,
At shoeing he would be the best,

Bow could also be God's tutor,
If modern tech is in his plan,
Bow could show him how to run his computer,
By transferring ranch records from the bottom of Dad's key can,

A lot of their wives have gone to join them including Mom,
I really can understand why,
To leave that bunch alone would be a time bomb,
The women might keep them from upsetting the Big Guy,

If any of you old timers still around,
Should find it time to leave your earthly nook,
Seeing as how you are Heaven bound,
If you want to find Dad I'll tell you where to look,

Look for a horse they say can't be broke,
Or a windmill in need of repair,
Or maybe someone slapping a mouthy bloke,
Chances are he might be there,

You might also look at the coffee shop,
Or at a football game,
Just look where the visiting will never stop,
Or from where some strangers came,

All in all God's ranch is in good hands,
I sure am satisfied,
As I still watch the sifting sands,
Twenty-five years after Dad died,

By: Mick Scarlett

Bill and Bessie Scarlett (1947)

FORWARD

Welcome to Volume Two of My New Beginning books,
"THE YOUNGEST MOUNTAIN MAN". Volume One, "THOSE
MAGNETIC SANDHILLS", has been out since August
of 1998.

Volume Two depict many of the same characters
in Volume one plus a few new ones, including
the main character. Teddy Springers situation
happens more in our great country than most of
us would like to admit.

Those people that advocate legalization of other
mind altering drugs besides alcohol need first
to admit the problems it creates. Next, they
need to multiply that by the problems more
legalized drugs would add.

It is easy to cure the problem in a fictional
story. It is not nearly as easy to cure it in
real life. Just ask a family that has been
destroyed by alcohol.

I hope everyone enjoys, "THE YOUNGEST MOUNTAIN
MAN". Volume Three is about two thirds written
at this time. It is called "A SOLDIER RETURNS"
and I hope you will watch for it in the future.

An old friend and I are currently working an
a nastalgic history of our sandhill area called
Gritta Ridge. Hopefully it will include
experiences of real life happenings by actual
people and many pictures. It should be very
interesting reading. We will call it, "RIDGE
KIDS".

Mick Scarlett

TABLE OF CONTENTS

Chapter 1

A TWELVE YEAR OLDS' DILEMMA

Teddy awoke with a start. Something had hit his bedroom wall with a crash and now he could hear his mother screaming and his dad's loud cussing. "Oh boy, here we go again Toby," he said. Toby, his faithful companion of the last two years, jumped on the bed and huddled by Teddy shivering nervously. "Don't worry boy, we won't try to interfere with their fight." Teddy tried to stop his parents fighting once before, and was rewarded with a hard slap from his drunken dad. When Toby came to his rescue, he had been kicked hard in the side. Toby was part German Shepherd, was medium sized and very defensive of Teddy.

The fight was continuing in the other room. Both of his parents were drunk and he knew they would continue to fight until they wore out, or passed out. Tomorrow would be another normal Sunday. Teddy had made himself a lunch so he could slip out quietly. He had found out it wasn't good to make the slightest noise on Sunday morning untilhis parents sobered up. He hoped it would be a nice day so he could spend most of it in the park. A note was already left for his mother in case she woke up and wondered where he was.

Things had been pretty good for the first six months after they had moved to Baltimore from Philadelphia. His parents didn't have many friends then and didn't party much. They spent more time as a family and for a while he actually thought things had changed. Eventually though, his father made new so called friends and they invited his parents to parties. At first only occasionally but now it was every Saturday night.

When they came home drunk, they always fought.
They were pretty good people when they were sober,
but drunk their personalities were one hundred
percent different. Teddy used to be able to
at least look forward to a baby sitter in
Philadelphia, but since he was twelve years old
and had his dog his folks figured he could stay
alone now.

By this time, the screaming and cussing
had started to taper off and Toby quit shaking.
Teddy found himself thinking of Ann Jorden.
He had fallen in love with her the first time
she babysat him. At the time he was six and
she was in high school. Ann was so full of energy
that there was never a dull moment when she was
around. She talked to him all the time. Teddy
smiled to himself as he remembered the times
 Ann took him to the riding stable. She was
so fun to be around and he wondered where she
was now. Her sister Ellen had babysat him a
couple of times but she was the exact opposite
of Ann. Ellen hardly paid attention to Teddy
and mostly talked on the phone or looked at herself in the mirror.

The noise had stopped coming from his parents
room now. Teddy took his flashlight and checked
the clock. Three a.m., that's about normal
thought Teddy as he snuggled under the covers
by Toby to try to get back to sleep. They awoke
again about seven thirty and dressed quietly.
With Toby he slipped out into the March weather.
It looked like a nasty day but he would rather
be outside in the damp cold than at home where
he might disturb his mom and dad. They walked
slowly towards the park, Teddy wondered how long
he could keep living like this. He hated it
and was sometimes afraid his dad wopuld really
hurt his mom. She was always beat up and even
went to the hospital once. It was after the
time ho and Tohy had tried to stop them form
2.

fighting. He knew she had lied to the doctors
as to what had happened.

They reached the park and went to the protection of the canopy over the big brick fire
pit where people could cook in the summer. It
started to rain and the wind was coming up.
Teddy and Toby found a place out of the wind then
Teddy opened his lunch sack for a snack. He
never forgot Toby either, half of the lunch was
for him. Toby had been his only salvation.

Suddenly an idea popped into his mind.
He had been reading about the westward movement
of the Pioneers in American History and was
fascinated by their persistence and how tough
they were. "Do you suppose we could manage to
go west on our own Toby?" he asked as the dog
ate half a sandwich. The idea ran through his
mind again and again. From that time on Teddy
knew he would leave someday but needed time to
figure out how and where to go.

Teddy was startled by a cheery hello from
Becky Downs. She was the first friend he had
made when they moved to Baltimore and even though
he had sworn that he hated girls a couple of
years ago it looked like he was changing his
mind. Becky was really nice. Toby ran to her.
She liked him as much as Teddy did. "Parents
at again?" Becky asked. "Yes," replied Teddy.
Becky was sure lucky, her parents didn't drink
at all and they were always doing things with
her and her little brother. "How do you stand
it?" Becky asked. Teddy had told her long ago
about the fights and how his parents screamed
and yelled and beat on each other. "It's getting
harder all the time." answered Teddy.

"I can trust you completely can't I Becky?"
asked Teddy. "You know you can," replied Becky.
"Well Toby and I have just made up our minds,
3.

we are going west as soon as the weather gets
better." Becky gasped. "How will you go?" she
asked. "I guess on foot," answered Teddy. No
one said anything for awhile. Finally Becky
broke the silence, "I would worry terrible about
you and Toby. What would you eat and where would
you stay?" "I haven't worked out all the details
yet," said Teddy. "I have to do something though
that is all there is to it." There was silence
again until Becky said, "I can understand that,
but I sure wish there was something else you
could do." "So do I," said Teddy, "but I have
no where else to go." "You don't even know anyone
out west do you?" asked Becky. "No, but I could
do all right I know I could!" exclaimed Teddy.
"Will you let me know before you leave?" asked
Becky. "Sure I will, in fact, I'll leave you
a note in our secret place if I leave in a hurry."
replied the determined young man. The rain had
stopped and the wind was blowing harder. "Why
don't you come to my house? It's too cold to
sit out here until you can go home," declared
Becky. Teddy hated to impose on his friends
folks but knew it would be miserable in the park
for the next four or five hours. They headed
for Becky's house with Toby trotting between
them.

"Hi Teddy!" exclaimed Becky's mother as
they entered the house. Becky must have told
her about his folks because she never did ask
about them. "Would you two like some hot chocolate?" asked Becky's Mom. Her name was Rose
and Teddy thought it was fitting. She was always
bright and cheery like a rose. They sat up
to the table as Rose mixed up hot chocolate for
them. Becky's little brother Bobby raced into
the room and right to Teddy. Teddy was his hero
and it embarrassed him a great deal the way the
little boy looked up to him. "Settle down Bobby,"
said Rose. "Sit up by Ted and you can have some
hot chocolate also". It always made Teddy feel

4.

so grown up when Rose called him Ted. She was
the only one that ever did except his dad when
he was mad and yelling at him. Becky's dad had
stayed at the church to help repair a broken
window so he wasn't home yet. Teddy found himself
thinking how nicee it would be to live in a family
like Becky's. I guess it just wasn't meant to
be he thought. Time flew by as Becky, Bobby
and Teddy played cards with Rose while Toby slept
on the floor. Finally, Teddy knew he had to
return home and see what the situation was there.
He stood to leave as Rose said, "Must you go
already Ted?" "Yes," he replied. "My parents
will be getting worried." Oh how he wished that
were the truth he thought as he left Becky's.

Teddy walked slowly home. It was almost
one p.m. and surely his folks would be up by
now. He entered the house quietly. His mother
was sitting by the heater in the kitchen drinking
coffee. She looked terrible. Her eyes were
red either from crying or being hit. She had
a large bruise on her cheek and hardly noticed
Teddy. As he walked by, she did manage to tell
him to be quiet and not wake his father. He
must have been pretty bad if he is still sleeping
thought Teddy. He went to his room after having
some crackers and tried to study. Unable to
concentrate, he began to write down a list of
things he would need if he headed west. He could
use his backpack that he had used in Boy Scouts
in Philadelphia. He had saved two dollars from
running errands for old Mrs. Jones next door.
She couldn't walk very good. He would need quite
a bit more money than that he thought. Sometimes
his mom had money in her purse after they had
been drinking and he was sure she never knew
how much was left. He hated to steal but he
would need at least twenty dollars before he
left. That sounded like a lot of money but he
had time to try to collect it as he wouldn't
be able to leave before the middle of April when
the weather was better. 5.

From that moment on, Teddy found himself thinking of leaving during every spare moment
that he had. He had difficulty concentrating
in school because his mind would wander to the
things he would need. He wanted to leave prepared. Once he was gone, he didn't plan to return.

One night after school, Teddy found a visitor
at his house when he came home from school.
It was none other than Ellen Jorden from
Philadelphia. Ellen had been in his parents
society circle in Philadelphia and had rode to
Baltimore with a friend to visit. Teddy wanted
to ask her a dozen questions about Ann but knew
his mother would get upset as she wanted to hear
all of the gossip Ellen knew from Philadelphia.
Teddy went to his room but sat quietly by the
door hoping to hear something about Ann. Finally,
Pat, teddy's mom, asked Ellen where Ann was.
"Oh!" exclaimed Ellen, "She married a rancher
in Nebraska. What a dreadful country." She
went on to say that Ann and Joe were both married
and living in the sandhills near the small town
of Milligan. Teddy quickly wrote the name of
the town down and instantly knew he had a destination when he left home. He listened quietly
as Ellen kept telling about the dreadful town
in the sandhills. Her, her mother, and their
maid had made the train trip out there twice.
They went out when Joe and Nancy were married
and eight months later when Ann and Andy were
married. The train ride was terrible she com-
plained. It took hours and hours to go almost
fourteen hundred miles. Oh boy, thought Teddy,
fourteen hundred miles was a long ways. His
mind was made up though. Things had gotten worse
around home in the last two weeks since he had
made up his mind to leave. He was wondering
if he would even last until the middle of April.
The more he listened to Ellen tell how terrible
the sandhills were the more he knew he wanted
to see them. He knew if Ann liked it out there
he would too. Ellen was telling Teddy's mom

6.

how there was no dress shop in Milligan and only
about two hundred people. "Of course," she said,
"Ann doesn't hardly ever wear a dress anyway."
Teddy laughed to himself as Ellen carried on
about how horrible it was. She was getting ready
to leave how but Teddy had heard enough. He
would make him a map in school tomorrow and put
the highways to Nebraska on it. He wrote down
highway two on his paper because Ellen had
mentioned how horrible it was being just gravel
and terribly dusty.

The next day in school Teddy found a map
of the United States and he drew out a rough
map with the highways that looked the best to
follow to Nebraska. He knew of course that he
couldn't walk right down the roads. He would
have to travel at night and stay off the road
even then unless there was no traffic. Someone
would sure report him if he were spotted. He
made two copies of his map. Milligan wasn't
on the map in Nebraska but he located highway
two and knew if he got that far, he would find
it. The teacher was asking for the assignments
to be handed in. Teddy had spent so much time
on his map that he wasn't quite done with his
assignments. He asked to stay after school and
finish. It was Friday and she would lower his
grade it it were not handed in until Monday.
He hurried to finish his work and rushed out
of school to try to get home before his mother
was upset with him. Becky was waiting for him
as he hurried out of the building. "You sure
have been keeping to yourself Teddy," she said
as she fell into step beside him. "I guess I
have a lot on my mind Becky," he replied. "Still
plan on leaving later on when the weather is
better?" She asked. "More determined than ever,"
he replied. "Isn't there anything else you can
do Teddy?" Becky asked. "I can't think of anything. I don't think my parents will ever get
help with their drinking problem." "When do
you think you will leave?" she asked. "I don't
7.

know but if I leave and don't get to talk to you I will leave you a note in our secret hiding place at the park." said Teddy. By this time, they had reached Becky's house and she turned in, "Be careful Ted." she called. That was the first time she had ever called him Ted. He hurried into the house as his mother called, "Kind of late aren't you?" "Yes Mom," he replied. "I was talking to Becky awhile after school." "I want your room cleaned up tomorrow and I will need you to help me clean the house tomorrow as your father and I are entertaining guests Saturday night," his mother replied. Oh great, thought Teddy. We would be expected to stay up in his room and then would have to help clean up the mess on Sunday. He really didn't mind cleaning up but usually his folks fought worse after they had a party in their house than when they went out. He had no idea why but just knew they did.

As usual, the party was a wild one. Teddy and Toby entertaained themselves by going over the supplies he had accumulated for his trip west. He was pretty well ready with his supplies. He didn't know what all he needed for sure but had accumulated a large package of beef jerky as he knew pioneers made jerky as it would keep. He had bart of a bag of dog food for Toby, crackers, matches in a small jar to keep them dry, one change of clothes, the ten dollars he had accumulated, and numerous other necessities. His backpack was stuffed. Toby seemed to sense that something was happening as he stayed close to Teddy when he was going over his supplies. He wished he had more money but hadn't been able to earn more or sneak any out of his mother's purse. Teddy dozed off for awhile but awoke as the last of the guests left. He almost dreaded to have the party get over as his folks would probably start their weekly battle.

8.

A loud crash told him that the fight was on. It sounded like the large window in the living room had been broken. Then he could hear his father yelling, "look at this mess, get it cleaned up now!" Pat screamed back, "it was as much your party as mine, you clean it up!" Now they were yelling and throwing things and he couldn't even understand them. He really didn't want to hear but couldn't get away from it. Finally, he heard his dad yell, "Get that damn kid down here. He can clean it up, he don't do anything else." It really hurt to hear his own dad say that even if he was drunk. Now he was yelling, "Ted, get down here now!" Teddy locked Toby in his room as his dad was violent towards the dog when he was drunk. He went downstairs. The front window was broken out and his mother was crying on the couch. "Clean this mess up and put something over that window!" his dad shouted. "He can't fix the window you idiot!" screamed Pat. "Shut up, you bitch!" yelled Teddy's dad. With that he shoved Teddy towards the window, grabbed Pat by the hair and dragged her across the floor. It was all Teddy could do to keep from trying to help his mother, but he knew he could be hurt seriously if he interfered. He tried to start cleaning up the mess but didn't know what to do. His dad shoved Pat into the bathroom and slammed the door. He returned to where Teddy was trying to clean up. "Hurry up Ted get that window covered!" shouted his dad. Teddy got a blanket from the next room and was trying to hang it over the curtain rod when his dad approached cussing wildly, bumped into the chair Teddy was on and he fell into the broken glass cutting his hand. "Get out of here worth-less. You are no better than your no good mother!" screamed the evil person that the alcohol had created in his dad's body.

Teddy ran up the stairs and into his room. He was crying violently as he shut the door.

9.

Toby was trying to lick his cut hand and his
face. Teddy just sat on the floor and cried
for about an hour. All the while, his dad was
trashing the house and yelling like a maniac.
 Finally, Teddy got control of himself and said
to Toby, "This is it. We have to leave as soon
as we can." He had wanted to leave in the evening
so he had all night to travel and get as far
as he could before daylight when he would have
to hide. It was already three a.m. and he didn't
see how he could get very far before morning.
Then he thought of the junkyard on the west edge
of town. If he could get that far, he could
hide there until Sunday night. He had to try
it. He quickly wrapped his bleeding hand up
and found his coat, gloves and cap. He also
pulled on his rubber boots. He had been keeping
them in his room ever since he had decided to
leave. It was a chilly night and it had been
raining earlier so he put his coat and hat on
to try and keep warm and dry. He slipped his
backpack on and peeked out the door. His dad
was still in the living room so he had to wait.
Then he thought of Becky. He slipped his gloves
off and found a pencil and paper.

     He wrote:

     Becky,

     Things have gotten out of hand here tonight. Can't
     take it any longer. Will try to get word to you some
     way later on.

                         Your friend, Ted

     He folded the note put it in his coat pocket,
slipped his gloves on and peeked out the door
again. The living room was empty. He slipped
out quietly and eased down the stairs. Toby
was close behind. No one was around as he eased

out the door and into the cool night air. Teddy
hurried to the park found the loose brick in
the grill, removed it, put in the note and replaced the brick. "Come on Toby," he said, "we
have to hurry."

They avoided the light areas and hurried
towards the junkyard. It was over four miles
and Teddy was really tired by the time they
reached it. He had brought his flashlight so
he shielded the light with his coat and used
it to help him find a dry car to crawl into.
Even though he was terribly weary, he and Toby
lay there a long time before either one of them
slept. Teddy had no idea how long it would be
before he had a place to call home again.

Chapter 2

WESTWARD HO!

Teddy woke up about two p.m. It was stifling hot in the old car as the bright sun shined through the windows. He opened the door slowly so it didn't make a noise. As he and Toby ate some crackers and beef jerky, the fresh air felt good. It would be a long time before dark so Teddy rummaged around in the old car to see what was left in there. He found nothing he could use, but did find an old car manual that he read through. As he read, he got sleepy again and dozed off. When he awoke this time, it was almost dark so he gathered up his pack. They slipped out of the juinkyard and headed west. There was still quite a few houses along the highway and an occasional street light so Teddy stayed in the shadows which made walking difficult. There was also quite a bit of traffic so they had to stay off the highway. He did recognize a sign that said highway fifty, which was the one he planned on following as far as he could.

Back at home, Teddy's mother was really getting worried. She had started calling different friends of his by mid-afternoon to see if he was with them. She finally went to her husband and told him how worried she was at six p.m. "Oh, he will be home by supper, you can bet on that, He is just staying away until the mess from the party is cleaned up." He had spent several hours putting in a new window and cussing whoever broke it out. Pat guessed he had no idea he had thrown a flowerpot at her and it went through the window. He either didn't know it or didn't want to admit it. Finally,

at nine p.m., they were both worried. Pat had
searched Toby's room and was really concerned
when she found his backpack, canteen, scouting
knife and a few other things missing. "You don't
suppose he ran away?" she asked Arlo her husband.
"He better not have or when I get my hands on
him I'll tan his backside good," he replied.
"Did you do anything to him last night after
the party?" Pat asked. "Hell no, I never saw
him after the party," He said either lying or
not really remembering. Finally, at ten Arlo
let his wife call the police. The police said
that usually most runaways return within two
days after they experience a couple of nights
away from home. He took Teddy's description
and told Pat he would tell everyone to watch
for him.

Meanwhile, Teddy was continuing westword.
As it got later, the traffic got thinner and
thinner until there was hardly any cars on the
road. Teddy and Toby finally risked walking
on the road surface and made much better time.
By the time the eastern horizon started to lighten
up, they had made several miles and were well
out of the suburbs of Baltimore. Soon traffic
started to pick up and Teddy knew he had to locate
a place to hide for the day. He was worn out
and his feet were sore. Finally in the growing
light he spotted some thick trees and brush.
He and Toby struggled into the thick undergrowth
scaring out a surprised rabbit. Teddy was so
tired he never even ate. He dug out his old
blanket and laid it on the ground after he cleared
off a small spot and was sound asleep as soon
as he lay down. Toby was tired also but would
have liked to have eaten some dog food before
he lay down. He looked longingly at the backpack
for a little while then curled up beside Teddy
and slept also.

Teddy finally woke up with hunger pains

about mid-afternoon. Toby was more than ready
to eat by then. Teddy rationed out Toby some
dog food and ate a healthy meal of beef jerky
and crackers. His supply looked awfully meager
after only two days. He guessed he wasn't very
good at rationing his food. Suddenly, a thought
occurred to him. How was he going to buy more
food if he couldn"t be seen in any of the towns?
Panic set in for a minute but Teddy told himself
he had to be calm. He would think of something.
Toby kept begging for more food but Teddy had
to tell him no. It would be a few more hours
before they could travel again and they would
eat a little before they left. Teddy wondered
if Becky had found his note yet. It would be
a couple hours before school was out he thought
as he looked at the pocket watch he had taken
from the drawer at home. He reminded himself
he better be sure to wind the watch because if
it ran down he would have no way of telling what
time it was to reset it. He didn't realize that
for the next few months of his life, time would
mean very little to him.

Meanwhile back in Baltimore, Becky sat nervously at her desk as their teacher introduced
a policeman to the class. Her mother had told
her on Sunday that Pat Springer had called looking
for Teddy. She wondered then if something had
happened and he had left home before he expected.
She didn't think too much more about it until
she arrived at school Monday morning and Teddy
wasn't there. The day seemed to drag on and
on. Becky wanted to get to the park to see if
there was a note there. Now there was a policeman
in the classroom and her heart was in her throat.

After the teacher introduced him, the policeman began to speak. "We have a missing persons
report on a Teddy Springer," he said. "I understand he was in this class and wondered if he
had mentioned to any of you that he might run
away. If so, did he say where he might go?"

14.

No one answered. Becky just stared at her desk
hoping no one could hear the thump, thump of
her heart like she could. The policeman spoke
again, "It's for Teddy's own safety that we
are asking you so if any of you remember of him
mentioning running away, please let me know."
He then thanked the class and the teacher and
left. "This is terrible," said Miss Carr after
the policeman had left. "Teddy could be in real
trouble. If any of you know anything please,
please tell me." Becky kept quiet. She couldn't
betray Teddy but hoped he was o.k. Finally the
final bell rang and school was out. Becky raced
as fast as she could to the park. No one was
there, so she slipped the loose brick from its
resting place. Sure enough there was a note.
Her heart pounded as she read what Teddy had
written. It must have really been bad at home
for Teddy thought Becky as she walked slowly
home. What do I do now she thought. It was
either betray Teddy or keep her promise. She
knew she would never betray him but it was going
to be hard. She said a short prayer for him
before she entered her house. Her mother met
her at the door. "Have you heard anything about
Teddy?" asked Rose, Becky's mom. "Only that
they think he might have ran away," replied Becky.
"Oh no!" exclaimed Rose, "Has he ever mentioned
running away to you Becky?" Becky had never
lied to her mother before. She guessed a little
white lie wouldn't condemn her for life. "No
Mom," said Becky. "I don't recall it anyway.
He did say it was getting worse when his parents
fought when they had been drinking." "Oh that
poor boy," said Rose. "I do hope he is o.k.,"
she continued.

Dark found Teddy and Toby back on the road
or rather in the ditch. They didn't dare walk
on the road until the traffic thinned out and
they would have time to hide if there was a
vehicle coming. It was slow going in the rough

ditch with no light to see by. They had to take
their time and before long Teddy's legs ached.
They weren't as bad as the first two nights though
and as the days passed, Teddy would find himself
stronger than ever. As they walked, Teddy stopped
to drink from his canteen. Toby drank from water
in the ditches but it didn't look appetizing
to Teddy. He had filled his canteen at a hand
pump in a park the last time but needed to refill
it again. It was a very dark noght and Teddy
couldn't see much more than a few feet ahead
of him. They stopped for a break near a farm-
stead. Teddy could hear the squeaking of a windmill somewhere in the dark. He had heard a windmill before since he had left so he was pretty
sure that was what it was. Knowing he would
have to have water, they started towards the
sound. The windmill was very close to the house
when they found it. Teddy carefully slipped
up to the tank and held the canteen under the
lead pipe. Just as the canteen was full, Toby
growled and suddenly a large dog began barking
furiously. Teddy froze in his tracks. Suddenly
the front light came on and the door opened
exposing a farmer in his nightclothes holding
a shotgun. "What is it Tag?" he asked. "Raccoons
in the chicken house again old boy," he continued.
Teddy had stepped behind a large gatepost and
stood quietly. The farmer walked within a few
feet of Teddy and Toby. Why the farmer didn't
shine his light that way Teddy never knew but
as soon as the farmer entered the chicken pen
Teddy and Toby hurried into the trees. When
they were in good cover, theystopped and Teddy
tried to breathe quietly. The farmer came from
the chicken pen and headed for the house. His
dog was still barking. "Settle down old boy,"
he said. "I think you scared off whatever was
out here." Teddy breathed a sigh of relief as
he and Toby headed for the road. It was late
now and little or no traffic was on the road.

16.

They took advantage of that and put a
couple of miles between them and the
farm place as quickly as they could.

The next five days went pretty smoothly
and although Teddy didn't know how far they had
came, he did know he could see the Appalachian
Mountains looking to the west. The terrain was
already geting rougher and a clear mountain creek
provided Teddy with plenty of water. The stream
didn't do much for their food supply though and
it was almost nonexistent by now. Toby fared
better than Teddy in the food department because
he ate various goodies that he found along the
road. None of them looked too appetizing to
Teddy though and they didn't always agree with
Toby either., Teddy had lost count of the days
he had been gone but when he woke up and dug
in his backpack he discovered his food supply
was gone. Toby looked at him pleadingly as he
dug around in the backpack, but Teddy had to
say, "Sorry old boy, it's all gone." It was
a long day with nothing to eat. The hunger pangs
kept Teddy awake most of the day but as night
arrived they headed back on their westward trip.
About morning, Teddy spotted the lights of a
small town. "Let;s get as close to that town
as possible Toby," said Teddy. He was hoping
he could figure out some way to buy some food
without anyone suspecting he was a runaway.
They stopped just about a quarter mile from the
town in a patch of tall grass. Teddy smoothed
out a spot and lay down his dirty blanket. As
it got light, Teddy could see that the tall grass
continued almost clear up to the street in town.
Teddy dug out his only change of clothes. They
had stayed clean but were wrinkled up bad. He
smoothed them out as best he could and put them
on. He smoothed out his hair that was really
getting long now and tried to wipe his face clean.

"You stay here Toby, I'll try to get us some food with this ten dollars," said Teddy. Toby whined as Teddy walked off but he knew he had to stay. Teddy crouched down in the tall grass and started towards town. He stepped out of the grass and onto the broken old sidewalk and tried to walk as natural as possible. Teddy entered a general store and walked to the counter. "Can I help you young fella?" a kindly old gent asked. "My folks and I are traveling to the mountains and they told me I could get some beef-jerky and crackers as I am always hungry," lied Teddy. The old man laughed and replied, "I was always hungry when I was your age too son. How much jerky do you want?" "Quite a bit," said Teddy. "I sneak my dog some once in awhile when the folks don't see me. They say it's too expensive for dogs." "It is pretty expensive dog food son," replied the storekeeper as he lay a large package of beefjerky on the counter beside a box of soda crackers. "I do have some new fangled dog food in ten pound bags if you want to try that." "If I buy it and Mom and Dad want me to bring it back, will it be all right?" Teddy asked. "Sure can, where are your folks anyway?" asked the clerk. "We camped in a tent in the park." said Teddy, thankful he had saw the park on his way into town. "That will be two dollars and ten cents," said the storekeeper. "That dog food is eighty cents but it's still cheaper than feeding your pet beefjerky," he continued. "Thanks," said Teddy as he lay three one dollar bills on the counter. He took his supplies and headed out the door. He tried not to hurry as he walked toward the edge of town. When he reached the park, he was only about a hundred feet from the tall grass. He looked back and the storekeeper was sweeping the sidewalk and watching him. He was glad he had looked back because if the old man had seen him sneak into the grass he might have become suspicious. Teddy walked into the park and made sure he was

18.

out of the storekeepers sight before he slipped
into the grass. He hurried as fast as he could
crouched down and soon he and Toby were eating
hungrily. "We must not eat too much Toby. I
don't know when I'll get a chance to do that
again," said Teddy. Feeling better, Teddy and
Toby both lay down and were fast asleep in no
time at all.

Back in Baltimore Teddy's mother was frantic
with worry. His dad didn't seem to be all that
worried but deep inside he knew he had mistreated
his son. Pat called the police station every
day at least twice to see if they had heard anything. She had quizzed Becky and Teddy's other
friends but had found nothing out. She knew
also that the drinking and fighting had driven
her son away and had vowed to never drink again.
It had the opposite effect on Teddy's dad. He
seemed to want to drink every night, then he
blamed his wife for driving Teddy away. The
quilt was weighing heavy on his shoulders.
Teddy's picture and description had been in all
the papers and everyone was amazed that he hadn't
been spotted yet.

Meanwhile, Teddy and Toby kept their westward
movement going every night. After being so hungry
before, Teddy managed to restrict his eating
better this time. They were getting higher and
higher into the Appalachians now and the rough
ground and rocks had taken their toll on his
shoes. The soles were worn through and his feet
were bloody at night when he stopped. He tried
stuffing extra socks into the shoes but they
were soon worn through. He had long abandoned
his rubber boots that he took with him the first
night, as they were so heavy. His food was gone
again and the situation was getting desperate.
They had plenty of water though. The mountain
streams were cold and clear. Teddy found a place
by the stream to hide, as day approached for

what seemed like the hundredth time. It was
close enough that he could let his sore feet
dangle in the water. It really felt good.
Finally, he crawled onto his blanket and was
soon fast asleep.

Several hours later he heard Toby growl.
Instantly he sat up. He cleared his eyes but
could see nothing. Toby kept growling though
and finally a buckskin clad figure stepped out
from behind a tree. "Hello there young man,"
said the stranger. He was obviously an Indian
and how long he had been watching Teddy he didn't
know. "Hello," said Teddy. "What brings you
into my mountains?" the man asked. "Just passing
through," replied Teddy. "Well no one passes
through here without having a meal with me at
my house so lets go. My name is Randy Silverfox
youngster, What's your handle?" said the Indian.
"Ted Springer and this is Toby," replied Teddy.
"Well get what"s left of them shoes on and lets
go," said Randy. Teddy hurriedly obeyed. He
could already taste the meal he had been promised.

A LESSON IN MOUNTAIN SURVIVAL

Teddy had to almost run to keep up with
Randy. The Indian took long even strides and
they coverd the ground rapidly. They were soon
at Randy's camp. It was more of a residence
than a camp. A fairly large area had been cleared
and a small log cabin stood in the cleared area.
Some hides were on stretchers and some were
already tanned and stacked in the cabin. Teddy
was fascinated with Randy Silverfox's camp.
When they first reached the camp, Randy told
Teddy to remove his wore out shoes. After Teddy
took his shoes off, Randy had started a rabbit
stew and proceeded to treat the sores on Teddy's
feet with some kind of salve. As he worked,
he told Teddy it was made of animal fat and juice
from different plants. While they waited for
the stew to get done, Randy asked Teddy where
he was headed. "Nebraska," replied Teddy.
"Nebraska!" exclaimed Randy. "I suppose you
realize how far that is," he continued. "Yes
sir I do," said Teddy. "Care to tell me why
your out here alone and half starved?" asked
Randy. For some reason Teddy trusted this tall
buckskin clad stranger. He proceeded to tell
him the whole story. After he had finished and
Randy had dished up some stew and threw some
scraps to Toby, Teddy asked, "Why do you live
out here and are you an American Indian?"

"Well," started Randy. "My life story is
almost the same as yours. My folks were hopeless
drunks. I finally left home when I was seventeen
and worked for a year. Then I lied about my
age and joined the service. I spent my time
in the service serving in Europe during the war.
I was captured and spent over two years in a
prison camp. After the war we came home heroes,

21.

but within a few weeks all was forgotten
and I was just an Indian again. No one
seemed to care, so I decided that if
they thought of me as just another Indian
that is what I would be. I moved out
here a year ago and have lived like my
ancestors ever since." Randy finished.
"Do you get lonesome?" asked Teddy.
"Sometimes I do, but would rather be
alone than put up with some people,"
replied Randy. "Who do you know in
Nebraska?" asked Randy. "Well Ann Evans
is the one I'm trying to find. She used
to babyset me years ago when her name
was Ann Jorden," said Teddy. "Jorden,"
repeated Randy... "I knew a Joe Jorden
in the service, in fact, he led the group
of men that saved our lives," he
continued. "Ann had a brother named
Joe," said Teddy. "He did serve in Europe
during the war because I heard his other
sister tell my mother that," said Teddy.
"Do you know him and what he looks like?"
asked Randy. I only saw him once in
Philadelphia but he was six foot one
or two, slim build, black hair, and dark
eyes," said Teddy. "Well I'll be I think
our Joe Jordens are one and the same," said Randy.
"It's a small world isn't it?" He continued.
"Did you say Ann's married name was Evans? I
knew an Andy Evans in the prison camp," said
Randy. "That's her husbands name," said Teddy
as Randy filled his dish with stew for the third
time. "This is amazing," said Randy. They ate
in silence for awhile. Finally Randy said, "you
need some new clothes and shoes and a few lessons
on survival on your own before you continue to
Nebraska." "You're not going to turn me in to
the police as a runaway then?" asked Teddy.
"No, I was in your exact shoes one time in my
life and if you walked all the from Baltimore

22.

on your own, there is no reason why you can't
make it to Nebraska with a little Indian ingenuity",
replied Randy. "Will you teach me how to survive
on my own?" asked Teddy. "I sure will, but it
will take some time," said Randy. "Time is about
all I have, "said Teddy as he patted Toby.
Randy laughed and proceeded to tell Teddy that
he would start sewing him buckskin clothes and
moccasins in the morning. He said there would
have to be lessons on how to make his own dried
meat and what plants he could eat. "Did you
ever shoot a rifle?" asked Randy. "No," replied
Teddy. "I don't have a gun nor the money to
buy one either," he continued. "Well, you will
have to learn to shoot starting timorrow," stated
Randy. "Until them sores heal on your feet,
target practice will be your primary class to
begin with. I have an old single shot twenty-
two that will be perfect to learn with," he told
Teddy. "Isn't shells expensive?" asked Teddy.
"Not twenty-two shells, besides I have several
hundred rounds that I will never use," said Randy.
 "How many shells in a round?" asked Teddy.
Randy laughed as he said, "One shell is one round
young man. Now you and Toby crawl into that
pile of tanned furs in the corner of the cabin
and get a good nights sleep. We have our work
cut out for us if we are going to make a mountain
man out of you before we send you to Nebraska."
Teddy gladly did as he was told. He felt more
secure with Randy than he had for years. It
wasn't long before he and Toby fell sound asleep.
Randy sat for a long time before he turned in
for the night. Many thoughts passed through
his mind of himself when he was teddy's age.
He hadn't left home until he was seventeen.
He had to give this kid a lot of credit for the
guts he showed in striking out on a fourteen
hundred mile hike at twelve years old. Well,
Randy vowed to see that Teddy was well trained
before he let him continue on. Then his thoughts

turned to Joe Jorden and Andy Evans. It was
incredible that their paths should cross again
through a twelve-year old runaway boy and his
dog. Well, he owed Joe his life and helping
this young fellow would be a small repayment
for what he had done. Finally, Randy drifted
off to sleep. Teddy and Toby weren't used to
sleeping at night but the security of Randy's
cabin and the comfortable sleeping conditions
made it easier. The fact that they were awake
most of the day before had real affect on the
two travelers. They slept soundly and never
awoke until they heard Randy around the campfire
and smelled breakfast. They came out of the
cabin to a beautiful mountain morning in the
Appalachians. "Good morning boys," said Randy.
"How did you sleep?" he continued. "Great,"
replied Teddy. Randy laughed easily and said.
"This mountain air is great for sleeping and
healing." They had a huge breakfast and Randy
doctored Teddy's feet again with his bear grease
ointment. They had already started to heal.
Next, Randy went into the cabin and brought out
a single shot twenty-two caliber rifle. "This
is the first gun I ever owned," said Randy.
"I have had it since I was twelve years old."
he continued. He handed it to Teddy along with
a box of shells and walked a short distance away
from camp, where he lined up about a dozen large
pinecones. When he returned, he showed Teddy
how to load the rifle and pull the hammer back.
Randy put the rifle to his shoulder squeezed
the trigger and one of the pinecones flew to
pieces as it skidded along the ground. Toby
jumped excitedly at the pop of the rifle. He
had never heard a rifle before. Randy handed
the rifle to Teddy and showed him how to line
up the sights and laughed as he jerked the trigger
and missed the pinecone by three feet. "You
just squeeze the trigger Ted," Randy said.

24.

While Teddy sat and practiced shooting,
Randy proceeded to make him a set of clothes
out of his supply of different tanned hides.
First he made him a pair of moccasins. He made
the soles out of double thickness badger hide.
The hide was tanned to be exceptionally tough.
Then he made him a buckskin shirt and pair of
pants. Teddy was amazed at how the buckskins
fit and how soft they were. His feet were still
tender but the moccasins felt good and he was
soon following Randy around when he wasn't
shooting. He and Toby were both eating good
and learning more than they ever had before.
Rand showed him how to strip and dry deer, rabbit,
and squirrel meat. He made Teddy learn to recognize different edible plants and plants that
would poison him. He showed him what plants
would heal wounds or burns. Teddy learned to
cook over a campfire and how to care for a gun.
Three weeks slipped by in a hurry. One morning
Teddy woke up and knew he must move on if he
was to get to Nebraska before winter. Randy
would be as sorry to see the young mountain man
go as he was to be leaving. When he told Randy
he had to leave, Randy just nodded. Then he
went to the cabin and brought out a backpack
he had made for him. It looked enormous to Teddy.
Randy started to fill it with supplies. Dried
venison, a special leather blanket treated with
bear fat to make it waterproof. Some of his
special salve for healing, extra moccasins and
extra soles with strips of leather to use in
putting them on with. This was just a few of
the supplies in the backpack. The very last
things to go in were three envelopes with stamps
and a short pencil, a bunch of rifle shells and
the gun Teddy had been practicing with. "I can't
take your rifle Randy," said Teddy as Randy took
the rifle apart and slipped it into the pack.
"I'm just loaning it to you Ted, I'll get it
back someday," said Randy. When it was loaded
Teddy slipped it on. He thought his knees would

buckle at first but finally stood with
it and walked around. "Wow!" exclaimed
Teddy. "This thing is heavy," he continued. "First rule of mountain traveling
is to not let your pack get light," said Randy.
He went on to tell Teddy that as soon as he
realized his pack was getting light , to stop
and replenish his supplies. "You get caught
in a storm without plenty of supplies and you're
in trouble," Randy told him. Randy replaced
Teddy's old canteen with a larger leather covered
one. He told him that he could usually drink
water from any running stream but to stay away
from still water unless he had to use it. They
went over everything Randy had taught Teddy in
the last weeks. Toby paced nervously seeming
to know they were leaving. Randy shot a rabbit
and watched Teddy clean it. It made him feel
good to know that Teddy had learned well.

   "I'm going the first thirty or forty miles
with you if you don't mind Ted," said Randy as
they had their last breakfast at the camp. "That
would be great," said Teddy. "You don't have
to unless you have a reason," he added. "Oh
I have a reason, I need some supplies and it
is about that many miles to the town where I
get them. It is in the direction you are going,"
replied Randy. Teddy told him he guessed that
was reason enough as they hoisted backpacks up
and started off. Randy said there was one more
important lesson for Teddy to learn. He had
drawn him a map of how he should travel to stay
in the mountains and forests as long as he could.
Randy told him if he stayed in the forests he
could travel most of the time in the day as he
would be in cover. That would make a big difference in how far he could get every day. The
route Randy had mapped out for Teddy would take
him southwest through West Virginia, south of
Charleston. Then he would go west through
Kentucky and the Daniel Boone National Forest.

From there he might have to travel nights until
he reached the Shawnee National Forests in the
southern tip of Illinois and then into the Mark
Twain National Forests of Missouri. Randy told
him that once he got there he would be in cover
most of the time. When he crossed into Missouri,
he would hit the Mississippi River and that would
be a problem. He would encounter several rivers
and streams on his way across all these miles
and Randy wanted to give him first hand instructions on crossing. The streams he could
wade if he knew to stay away from the swirling
holes that might be deep. The rivers were a
different story. He would have to impress upon
Teddy their danger.

They were covering ground rapidly and Teddy
was struggling to keep up. By mid-afternoon
they had coverd over fourteen miles and were
on the edge of a pretty large river. Randy
started Teddy's lesson immediately. They found
a camp and left their backpacks. Randy took
Teddy up the river several hundred yards, pointing
out several dangerous places to try to avoid.
Randy had a canoe to cross this river with but
he knew that Teddy would encounter several rivers
and would have no canoe waiting for him there.
He showed Teddy how to select four eight foot
logs and strap them together with leather straps
like he had packed in Teddy's backpack. They
trimmed the logs with hatchets that Randy had
also provided. They strapped the logs together
and then found a long slender pole to pole across
the river with. "It's hard to tell how long
it will take you to pole across a river Teddy,"
said Randy. Always work your way up the river
at least as far as we did today. If you see
any rapids or falls, be sure to either work above
them a long ways or below them until you have
plenty of distance to pole across while the stream
carries you, without hitting and dangerous spots.

By this time, it was evening and they headed
back to camp. The next morning, Teddy hoisted
his backpack on and they went up to the log raft
they had made. Randy explained what Teddy was
to do. First they strapped his pack in the middle
of the raft, then eased it into the stream.
Toby perched in front of the pack while Teddy
sat behind with one leg on each side. Randy
explained that he had a canoe further down the
stream and would join Teddy on the other side
as soon as he was safely across.

Finally Randy gave Teddy the go ahead signal
and Teddy pushed the raft into the stream with
his pole. They hit the rushing current and Teddy's
heart was in throat. He kept using his pole
to push them further across as they were swept
down stream. Randy ran along the other shore
shouting instructions. "Don't get tangled in
that brush near the other shore," shouted Randy.
Teddy quickly used his pole to push them back
into the middle of the river to avoid the brush.
Finally after what seemed like an hour, they
were nearing the far shore. "Pick out a place
where the banks not too steep and run her ashore,"
shouted Randy. Teddy gave one last shove and
the raft hit ground. Toby immediately jumped
ashore followed closely by Teddy. Teddy kept
ahold of the raft and pulled it up on the shore
further so he wouldn't lose his pack. After the
raft was safe, he flopped on the grass as he
was completely winded. Randy let out a whoop
and them yelled, "pull the leather bindings
off of the logs and carry them on your shoulders
to dry. I'll grab my pack and come across in
my canoe. Meet me down the stream about three
hundred yards." Teddy struggled to his feet
and done as he was told. Before long they were
together again and after a short rest, they headed
west. After the leather straps had dried, Randy
made Teddy add them to his pack. There was -

already a set in his pack but Randy said if he
ever lost a raft, he would have a spare set of
bindings.

Randy shot a rabbit about mid-afternoon
and they had rabbit stew for supper that night.
They covered ground rapidly the next day and
camped next to the town Randy would get supplies
in by that evening. The next morning, Teddy
and Toby waited while Randy went to town for
supplies. When he returned, he put a small packet
of salt in Teddy's pack saying, "This will give
the rabbit stew a little flavor until it's gone."
Randy went on saying as he put the twenty-two
together that he had given Teddy, "Now that your
used to that pack you better carry this rifle
ready to use. Remember to always eat fresh meat
if you can and save the dried meat until game
is scarce." "Here take the rest of my money
for all you have done for me," said Teddy as
he handed Randy the few dollars he had left.
"No I don't want your money Teddy, you don't
owe me any thing for what I have done," replied
Randy. Even though when Randy wasn't looking
Teddy stuck the money into Randy's pack.

The sad moment had come. Randy reached
into his pack and pulled out a large bundle.
"You might think this is rediculous, but here
is a coat I made you. You will find wrapped
inside, gloves, tall moccasins, and a fur cap.
It is extra weight but sould you not make your
destination by winter it will look pretty good,"
said Randy. By this time, Teddy's pack didn't
seem nearly as heavy. He was getting stronger
by the day. Randy also gave him two letters
to deliver to Joe Jorden and Andy Evans when
he found them. They shook hands and Teddy and
Toby turned west while Randy headed back east.
There was a catch in Teddy's voice as he thanked
Randy for everything he had done. "I'll take

29.

good care of your rifle and get back to you as soon as I can," he said as they departed company.

Chapter 4

FACING A TOUGH TIME

Back in Baltimore, Teddy's mom had all but given up on ever seeing her son again. She had slipped into a deep depression. Meanwhile, Arlo had turned even more to alcohol and was on the verge of losing his job. His boss was concerned because Arlo Springer was his best architect and hated to see the alcohol ruin his career. Mr. Goodwin knew Doctor Hardin the Springers' family doctor, so he took it upon himself to give him a call. "I'm calling out of concern for the Springer's," said Mr. Goodwin. "I was hoping you could help me convince them to seek counseling as this disappearance of their son is tearing them apart," he continued. "I understand and am very concerned my self," replied Dr. Hardin. He continued, "I haven't had an opportunity to see Mr. Springer but Mrs. Springer needs more counseling for her depression and maybe should be hospitalized for awhile." Mr. Goodwin then told the doctor he would try to talk to Arlo about their problem. Doctor Hardin thanked him as they hung up.

Mr. Goodwin decided to go right to Arlo and lay it on the line. He found him at his drawing table where he had produced very little usable work in the last weeks. "Arlo I understand how bad things are for you right now," said Mr. Goodwin. I think you need to take some time off and try to get some help coping with this situation," he added. Arlo sat and stared for a few minutes. Finally he said, "I caused my son to leave Mr. Goodwin and now I have to pay the price." "It will do no good to punish yourself for past mistakes Arlo. What you need to do now is get yourself pulled together. How

31.

is your wife standing up?" asked Mr. Goodwin.
"Not good," replied Arlo. "Well for her sake
and for your son when he is located you need
to get a hold of yourself. Your not doing any
good in the condition your in," said Mr. Goodwin.
I recommend you both go together to see your
Family doctor and try to regain your health,"
he added. Arlo nodded slowly as he gathered
up his drawing tools. He left the office and
went to his car. It was all he could do to pass
the two bars he had been frequenting every
evening. He entered the house and found Pat
sitting staring at the phone as usual. He sat
down beside his wife and took her hand. "We
need to try to get through this together," he
said. "Mr. Goodwin made me see that today and
I know he is right. We are both to blame for
Teddy leaving but we need to straighten out our
lives so that if we get a second chance to be
parents to Teddy we are able to do it," Arlo
continued. Pat burst into tears as she hugged
her husband. "What will we do?" she cried.
"I'll call Doctor Hardin right now," said Arlo.
"Maybe he can see us yet this afternoon," he
continued. While Arlo called the doctor's office,
Pat tried to get herself together. The recep-
tionest said they could come in about four p.m.
and the doctor would see them.

Pat and Arlo Springer looked terrible when
Doctor Hardin entered the room. The devastation
of knowing they had driven Teddy away had taken
its toll. As they talked, Doctor Hardin convinced
them that no matter what their mistakes in the
past they would be of no help if Teddy was located
and they were in the shape they were in now.
"What can we do," asked Arlo. "Are you ready
to take drastic steps to kick the alcohol habit?"
asked Dr. Hardin. "I'll do anything," said Arlo.
"How about you Pat?'" asked the doctor. "I'll
do whatever you say," Pat said quietly. While
the doctor made arrangements to admit Pat into

the hospital and Arlo to alcohol treatment center, they talked for the first time. in weeks.

"Why did it have to come to this before we could see our problems?" said Arlo. "I don't know," replied Pat. "Well I have my mind made up," said Arlo. "I want to get straightened out more than anything in the world," he continued. "That makes two of us," said Pat.

Dr. Hardin returned and told them the plan. Pat would be admitted to the hospital for counseling and tests. Arlo would spend four weeks in an alcohol rehabilitation unit. They could see each other every few days and talk by phone. He told them that the police would be notified and given phone numbers of where they could be reached if Teddy was located. They both thanked him and headed for home to pack their personal necessitites. While they were at home, the phone rang. It was Mr. Goodwin. "Did you get in to see the doctor?" he asked. "Yes," said Arlo. "We are both going to try to get help," he added. "That's great," said Mr. Goodwin. "I want you to know that your paycheck will keep coming for the next month while you are in rehab," he continued. Arlo's voice caught as he thanked his boss profusely. They both hoped that a month from now they would be on their way to renewed health.

Chapter 5

ON THEIR OWN AGAIN

Far away in Kentucky their son whom they wouldn't even recognize, was pushing his way west. He and Toby were getting into the mode of traveling again. After they had left Randy, Teddy had been lonesome for a few days but he was getting used to the mountain man life again. Of course, he had Toby and that helped considerable. Teddy had fashioned a strap to carry the coat, hat, and mittens that Randy had made him take along. He had started carrying the rifle ready for action and all the target practice had paid off. Only twice so far he had eaten dried meat. Otherwise, he had been able to shoot fresh meat every day. He had eaten turkey, rabbit and squirrel. He had found some of the plants that Randy had taught him to pick out. He could either cook his meals in the tin pot Randy had given him or on a stick over the fire.

It hadn't been all great though. It had rained for three days straight and even though Randy had treated his leather clothes with his famous bear grease, they eventually got wet. The last day of rain had been a miserable one until he had found a protected ledge where it was dry. He built a fire under the ledge so that the smoke would spread out and not be noticed. The wet wood smoked quite a bit at first but finally dried out and he had a good fire. He cleaned the squirrel he had shot and started it roasting over the fire. Then he pulled his wet buckskins off and hung them on a branch over the fire. The only thing he had kept from his old pack was his old blanket from home. He wrapped up in it near the fire and thought of his Mom, Dad, and Becky. He would like to let

them know he was all right but no way did he
want to go back. Toby curled up next to him
near the fire and slept. When the squirrel was
done, they made a quick meal of it. It was
getting towards evening by now and Teddy decided
to unwrap the coat that Randy had made him as
it had gotten wet also. It was a beautiful coat
and inside it was mittens, long moccasins, and
a fur hat. He turned his buckskin clothes so
the wet side was to the fire and hung the fur
coat up beside them. Suddenly from the corner
of his eye he saw a movement. It was about three
feet away and as he turned he saw a giant rattle
snake. The snake felt his presence at the same
time Teddy saw him and he coiled to strike. The
instant it took him to coil was all Toby needed.
He dived at the snake and just by luck caught
him just inches behind the head. Had he caught
him any further from the deadly fangs he would
have been bitten and surely died. He shook the
snake furiously but didn't release his hold.
He shook so hard with his ferocious hold that
he tore the head clear off. Toby dropped the
head and it lay thrashing on the ground. "Stay
back!" shouted Teddy as Toby approached the moving
head. Randy had told him of a beheaded snake
biting a man in its death thrashing. Toby obeyed
and Teddy finally threw the head from the area
with a stick. Teddy was still shaking as he
picked up the remainder of the snake and tossed
it away. Randy had shown him how to skin and
clean a snake but he was too shook up to try
it now. He had gotten lax as this was the first
ratler he had encountered. Randy had always
told him to use the leather poncho when he rested
or slept. He had shown him how to fold the edges
so snakes couldn't get next to him at night.
They couldn't strike him through the leather
poncho. He hadn't worried much as Toby usually
warned him when anything moved, but the snapping
and popping of the fire must have covered up

the big snakes approach. Teddy scratched the
faithful dog's ears as he thanked him for saving
his life. He replenished the firewood supply
and restoked the fire. It took quite awhile
for him to settle down after the snake incident
but he finally slept soundly.

The next morning dawned clear finally and
Teddy felt good with dry clothes and the sun
shining on him. Day after day passed until the
trees started to thin out. He looked at the
rough map that Randy had made. It looked like
this would be the first clear area on the map.
He started traveling at night and sleeping during
the day. This cut into his dried meat supply
as there was no chance to shoot fresh game at
night. He did manage to shoot a rabbit as he
was resting during the day. He did not have
a good cover to cook it in so he waited until
dark and built his fire in a hole so it wouldn't
be spotted. The roast rabbit tasted good after
several days of dried meat.

After five or six nights walking, they
crossed a well traveled road that must have been
the one that led north to Charleston. After
that, it was so many nights walking without daytime cover that Teddy was almost out of dried
meat and was getting worried. Finally in the
distance he could see hills with trees on them
and pushed harder. He soon entered the Daniel
Boone National Forest and felt right at home.
He shot two rabbits and a turkey right away and
he and Toby both ate their fill. The next morning
when he hoisted his backpack up he realized how
light it was. He remembered Randy's warning.
The fact that he had eaten most of his dried
meat had lightened it some but the main reason
it was light was because he had gained so much
strength from carrying it all those miles. Randy
had made his buckskins plenty big but Teddy was

36.

slowly filling them out more and more. Well,
Teddy thought as he headed deeper into the forest,
I better look for some game and try my hand at
drying meat. He knew that meant staying put
for several days in one place but it was something
he had to do. He knew that according to Randy
there would be open country between these trees
and the Ohio River. The Ohio River, he thought,
there would be quite a challenge. He had waded
several streams and had rafted across two wider
rivers so far but Randy had told him not to
challenge the Ohio on a raft. He had told him
to follow it until he came to a bridge and try
to cross unnoticed in the dark. Well, he would
worry about that when he faced it. Later that
day, he came upon a small clear lake and laughed
at the face staring back at him from the clear
water. He didn't see Teddy Springer. He saw
a dark skinned lad with black fuzzy whiskers
ever so slightly noticeable and long hair almost
halfway to his houlders. "I don't know how anyone
would recognize me Toby. I don't even recognize
myself," he said to his faithful companion.

Once deep into the forest again, Teddy
decided to find a base camp to hunt from. It
had to be a good camp near water. They would
be there at least a week. They traveled several
miles until they crossed a clear cold stream
that both Teddy and Toby could jump across.
Not too far on the west side of the stream, he
spotted what looked to be an ideal base camp
to Teddy. It was protected on three sides by
large rocks and heavy trees protected the other
side. In fact, Teddy probably would have walked
right by it if he hadn't shot and wounded a
rabbit that ran into the thick under brush.
When he shed his pack and crawled through the
thick brush to retrieve his supper, he found
himself standing in the perfect camp. There

was a large tree in the middle of the little
clearing. He would dig a fire pit under the
tree to dry his meat. No one would see the glow
at night and in the daytime the leaves of the
tree would spread the smoke out so it wouldn't
be noticeable. "I sure hope it don't rain in
the next few days," Teddy said to Toby as he
located a better entrance to his camp and
retrieved his pack. They proceeded to set up
camp. Teddy spent more time than usual, after
he had the rabbit cooking, building some protection. He chopped branches from some of the
trees and built him a small hut between two large
rocks. "Hope no more rattle snakes stop to
visit," he told Toby as he smoothed out the ground
for his bed and spread the leather poncho out
with his worn out blanket on top.

Teddy found himself wondering if there would
be plenty of game around for him to hunt. He
hated to shoot a deer as too much would go to
waste. Besides, he thought, to get close enough
to a deer with his twent-two would be pretty
tricky. A large turkey or several rabbits and
squirrels would be better.

Teddy and Toby made a meal of the cooked
rabbit and Teddy cleaned out his backpack. He
cleaned the little rifle just as Randy had shown
him as his livelyhood rested directly with the
firearm. Finally, he was satisfied that his
camp was in order and the two travelers crawled
into their hut, wrapped up, and were soon sound
asleep.

Daylight the next morning found Teddy and
Toby far from camp. Randy had told him to never
hunt near a permanent camp as you chase all your
game away. He had said it was all right to shoot
a meal now and then around camp as that wouldn't
spook everything away but if you hunted constantly

near camp you would soon find yourself walking
a mile to just fetch one meal. It was beautiful
country and Teddy was just enjoying the scenery.
He always hated killing animals but his and Toby's
survival depended directly on his ability to do just
that. Randy had told him that controlled hunting
was good for wild animals. It would break up
bunches and scatter them over larger areas.
He said that this also limited inbreeding and
made for better game. As he walked, he marveled
at how much Randy knew about animals and the
forests. "I don't believe we would have made
it much further if we hadn't ran into Randy,"
he said to Toby. The little dog looked at him
as if he understood every word he said. By noon,
Teddy had bagged a large turkey and two rabbits.
In fact, the turkey was so big that he decided
to head back to camp. He tied a piece of leather
between the turkey's legs and slung it over his
shoulder. That was another trick Randy had shown
him. When they were in camp, Teddy cleaned the
Two squirrels and put them on the fire to cook
along with some tuber plant roots he had found.
While they cooked, he cleaned and stripped the
turkey meat and laid the strips on the green
branches tied together with strips of green bark.
Next he placed his drying rack above the fire
so the heat would start to dry the meat. It
had to be high enough so the meat wouldn't
actually cook and his drying rack wouldn't burn.
He found his protected camp to be ideal for this
process. The wind wouldn't bother blowing the
heat one way or the other. If it hadn't been
well protected, he would have constantly had
to be moving the rack into the heat. When the
meat was on the rack, it looked like enough to
fill his pack but he knew as it dried it would
shrink and only be about half as much as there
was now. It would take another day of hunting
with luck to have enough meat. With good drying
conditions four or five more days would be

required to get the meat dry enough. Randy had
shown him how to cut into the strips to make
sure they were dry. One strip that wasn't dry
could ruin a whole batch. He just as well spend
an extra day drying Randy had said rather than
have to stop and do it all over again.

Six relaxing days later found Teddy and
Toby breaking camp. Teddy had bagged another
smaller turkey and two nice fat rabbits. He
had dried all of the meat for his pack. Besides
they had eaten well on all the fresh game Teddy
had shot.

Teddy stayed in the forest for several more
days. He crossed another major highway that
wasn't on his map and continued westward. The
trees thinned out but cover was sufficient for
daytime travel although game was less plentiful.
They made good time though, sometimes up to twenty
miles a day. Teddy had to replace the soles
on his moccasins twice but still had several
spare soles left in his pack. His feet were
so calloused and tough by now that he could have
almost went bare foot. After the cover was no
longer sufficient for daytime travel, they returned to their nightime schedule. Teddy had
learned an important lesson by now. When he
was fortunate enough to shoot fresh meat he cooked
it thoroughly then saved part of it for the
next couple of days. This conserved his dried
meat. He also found some plants that were edible
which helped his food supply. For several days
in one stretch they hit no natural water so had
to rely on sneaking water from wells whenever
they could.

Teddy had again lost track of time but knew
it must be mid-summer. He figured it was early
to mid-July when he watched the sunrise over
the Ohio River Vally. For the next couple of

days they traveled along the Ohio River.
Teddy used some of the fishing supplies, mainly
hooks and string, that Randy had given him.
He had no luck though so had to rely on his rifle
for his meals. Finally he spotted an old train
tressel crossing the river. Closer inspection
told him that it was no longer used but looked
stable. He would camp on the Kentucky side of
the river and cross at first light so he wouldn't
be spotted on the tressel in the daylight. The
crossing went well, once he convinced Toby that
it was safe. They traveled west in what is now
Hoosier National Forest until they hit another
major river. Randy had it on his map but couldn't
remember the name. Teddy found out later that
it was the Wabash River. They were now in
Illinois and the Shawnee National Forest. Daytime
travel was great here and they were covering
mile after mile until one day about noon Teddy
spotted a jeep hidden well into the trees. There
were no roads around and the jeep was obviously
hidden as branches had been laid on top of it
and stood up along the sides. As Teddy stood
some distance away trying to figure out what
was going on, he faintly heard voices coming
from somewhere on the other side of the jeep.
He backtracked a short distance away, removed
his pack and coat bundle and told Toby to stay
by the pack. He then proceeded to sneak toward
the voices. After much patient stalking, downwind
like Randy had taught him, he was close enough
to over hear the three men seated on a log.
They were counting a huge sum of money that they
had apparently dumped from a canvas bag laying
near by. After a fashion, one of the men almost
shouted, "One hundred and fifty thousand dollars!"
"Shut up you fool, someone will hear you," said
another of the men. "Who would hear us out here?"
asked the third man. "That's right, who would
hear us?" asked the one who had shouted. "You
can't be too careful,"

41.

said the man that seemed to be the leader of the group. "Well we have nearly fifty thousand each, let's put it back into the bag, No since dividing it until we are ready to split up," he continued.

They gathered up the maney, stuffed it in the bag, and talked about the shocked look on the clerk's face when they had pulled the gun on him. With that staement Teddy knew he had stumbled onto the hide out of three robbers. He listenen intently. "Well it's time to cele- brate," said the apparent boss, as he pulled three bottles of whiskey from the jeep where he had just stashed the money. As they started drinking heavily, Teddy knew from experience that it wouldn't be long before they were passed out. He crawled slowly back to where Toby and his pack were and began forming a plan in his mind. A little excitement would do him good he thought. He and Toby ate some jerky and after about an hour and a half when the laughing and shouting was almost completely silent from the direction of the bank robbers, Teddy told Toby to stay again and again approached the jeep. He crawled to where he could see the three men sleeping on the ground. They had drank all of the alcohol it seemed and were now sleeping it off. First Teddy crawled to the far side of the jeep. He pulled his hunting knife out and cut off one of the valve stems. The hissing air was louder than he expected and it scared him for an instant until he saw that the men never moved. He then cut off the remaining valve stems and picked up the bag of money. When he was back to his pack and Toby, he sat down to decide what to do. Finally he decided he needed a good hiding place for the cash until he could get word to the owner of the money, which he knew was a bank in St. Louis. The banks name

and address were stamped on the bag. He took
out his pencil and one of the three stamped
envelopes that Randy had put in his pack. Teddy
copied the name and address from the cash bag
onto the envelope. Next he assembled the army
shovel that he caried and off he and Toby went
to bury their treasure. Twenty steps straight
south of one of the largest trees in that area
was a huge rock. That looked like as good a
hiding place as any to Teddy so he headed towards
it.

After burying the sack of money and covering
it good, he sat for a few minutes just looking
over the ground so he could draw a treasure
map. To the north and almost in line with the
tree several miles away was a tall tower.
Probably a radio tower thought Teddy. He went
back to his pack after putting a smaller rock
on top of the big rock and drew up his treasure
map on one of the pieces of writing paper Randy
had given him.

It looked pretty rough when he was done
but he was sure he could find the money again
if no one else could. After that was done, he
dug a good sized fire pit. He put dried branches
in the bottom and lit it on fire. Over these
he laid green grass and leaves. There was no
wind and he had picked a spot in a clearing that
was rocky with hardly any flammable material
for a good distance. He hoped the smoke would
bring someone and they would find the bank robbers.

Next he packed up and proceeded to put as
many miles between him and the bank robbers as
he could. Two days later found him just north
of a small town and overlooking the mighty
Mississippi River. It was another of the big
three rivers that Randy had warned him about.

He laughed out loud as he wondered what had
happened to the three men when they came too.
He had been able to see the signal smoke all
the rest of the day and just before dark it had
suddenly went out. He was sure that the men
had either found it after they sobered up and
put it out or someone else had found it.
After he made camp that night he took out the
envelopes and writing paper and proceeded to
write three letters. On the back of the map
he wrote:

> Dear Sirs:
>
> I seemed to have come upon three appar-
> ent bank robbers while traveling.
> Proceeded to wreck their transportation
> and resteal your money from them while
> they slept off the effects of the
> alcohol that they used to celebrate
> their good fortune. Have buried the
> money and drawn you a rough map on
> the back of this letter so you can
> hopefully find it.
>
> Yours truly,
> Ted and Toby

Next he wrote to his parents:

> Dear Mom and Dad,
>
> I hope my leaving the way I did wasn't
> too stressful on you. I just couldn't
> stand to stay and see what the drinking
> was doing to you. I hope my leaving
> makes you realize how bad it was getting
> around there and helps you straighten
> out your lives. No matter what, I love
> you and always will. I will write again
> when I reach my destination.

44.

                    Your Son and his faithful dod,
                         Ted and Toby

Finally he wrote to Becky:

    Dear Becky,

    You will never believe where I am and
    where I have been. As near as I can
    tell I am just east of the Mississippi
    River in Illinois. I will try to cross
    tomorrow and proceed on to Nebraska.
    Someday I hope I can tell you first hand
    all of the experiences I have had and
    everything I have learned. My main
    teacher was an Indian by the name of
    Randy Silverfox. He taught me to not
    fight nature but learn to live with it.
    So far it has worked and if everything
    goes well, I will reach Nebraska before
    winter. That is where I plan to stop.

                         Your friends,
                         Ted and Toby

    ps. Tell your folks hello. I also wrote
        To my Mother and Father.

    Well, Teddy thought, as he settled down to sleep. To-
morrow I'll find a rural mailbox to mail my letters in and
then look for a way across the Mississippi River into Missouri.
He chuckled again to himself as he remembered
the three drunken bank robbers and wondered what
happened to them. Then he went over in his mind
the instructions Randy had given him. He
remembered him saying clearly. Cross into the
lower part of Missouri. Then head northwest
until you hit the Missouri River. Follow it
to Kansas City. Randy had told him that once
he reached Kansas City to keep following the
Missouri River but to also watch tor empty cattle

                         45.

trucks heading west into Nebraska. He
had said it should be fall by the time
he reached Kansas City and the ranchers
from the sandhills would be sending their feeder
cattle to the eastern farmers by that time.
If he was lucky, he could sneak aboard an empty
truck headed back for more cattle and cover lots
of miles in a short time. Teddy found himself
wondering how Randy knew so much about almost
everything as he finally went to sleep.

Chapter 6

LIFE IN THOSE SANDHILLS AT TEDDY'S DESTINATION

Hanks laughter rang from the living room.
"What in tarnation is so funny," asked Em from
the kitchen where she was preparing one of her
enormous suppers. Ann, Andy, and Joe and Nancy
were coming out for supper so the men could decide
how to market the yearlings this fall. Hank
came into the kitchen still laughing. "I was
listening to the national news on my new radio
and am amazed at how stupid some people are,"
he said. He had bought a new electric radio
after the Rural Electric Association had finally
brought power in about a month ago. What change
that had brought to the sandhills. "Don't talk
that way about people, your no Einstein yourself,"
said Em. "I'm not stupid enough to steal one
hundred fifty thousand dollars and then get drunk
and let someone steal it from me," said the old
man.

He went on to explain that according to
the news, authorities in Illinois had arrested
three apparent bank robbers. It seems a game
warden had spotted smoke in a secluded area and
he and a deputy sheriff had driven out to investi-
gate. When they arrived, they found what seemed
to be an intentionally set signal fire. While
they were extinguishing it, they heard a commotion
nearby and discovered a jeep with four flat tires
and three men. Two of the men had tied the third
to a tree with a rope, dropped his pants, and
were throwing cactus at his backside. from what
they could get from the three men, who were still
somewhat drunk, they had robbed a bank in St.
Louis then hid in the hills. After consuming
a bunch of whickey to celebrate, and passing
out the unfortunate one that was tied to the

tree had come to and walked a short distance
into the trees to relieve himself. When he
returned, the other two had awaken to discover
the flat tires and missing money. They had accused
the early riser of hiding the money and flattening
the tires to make it look like someone else had
done. it. They were in the process of trying
to torture the truth out of him when they were
arrested. "It took the warden and deputy an
hour to pull the cactus spines from the guys
rear end," laughed the old rancher. "Did they
find the money?" asked Em. "No it was no where
around," said Hank. At that time, Ace began
to bark as a car was approaching. "Go let the
kids in Hank," ordered Em. "Yes Mamma," said
Hank as he went to the door. Andy and Ann were
just walking over from where theylived. The
old bunkhouse had been remodeled into a house
when they were married. "Come in!" shouted Hank
to the four. They entered the house under Ace's
escort. They were no more than in the house
and Hank had to relate the bank robber story
to them. When he finished, Em said, "him and
his radio, sometimes I think I could leave and
he would never miss me." "I would realize you
were gone at mealtime," joked the old man. Everyone laughed as they sat down to what looked more
like a Thanksgiving dinner than a normal ranch
supper.

Ace took his normal position beside Hank
and usually fared better than anyone as far as
getting something to eat. Ann was the only one
that could coax the dog from his masters side.
She loved to tease her father-in-law almost as
much as he loved to tease her. From the first
time they met it had been a running contest to
see who could shut the other one up. Neither
had succeeded for very long at a time. They
loved to ride together and Ann could work as
hard as anyone. She had developed an uncanny

48.

ability to know when things were amiss on the ranch. In fact, she had been correct so many times no one even questioned her anymore when she felt like something was wrong. One time when two windmills had broken down, almost simultaneously right after they had been checked, and left the spring calving cows out of water, she felt something wrong and finally convinced the men to check the pasture two days before they normally would have. It had happened so often since then that Hank had taken to calling her his bewitched daughter-in-law. When ever he would really get to badgering Ann, Em would remind him of the fact that her intuitions had saved his life. The old man insisted he would have survived but no one else did and down deep he did believe she was very special.

It happened one nice day in July when Hank had rode out alone with his lunch to check pastures. By ten o'clock a rain storm had came up and Ann had a feeling that the old rancher was in trouble. This was before she had proven herself as a predictor of trouble on the ranch so when she told Andy of her fears for Hank he brushed it off. He told her that Hank had his slicker and had weathered many a storm. Besides, Ace was with him. Ann had asked if Ace would leave Hank if he was hurt and come home for help. Andy had said no he probably wouldn't. Finally after threatening to go looking herself, Andy and Joe had agreed to go. By this time, the rainstorm had become so intense that the wipers wouldn't even clear the windshield on the old pickup. When they came upon Hank's horse and no sign of Hank or Ace, silence fell on the group. Andy grabbed the bridle reins and looked the horse over. Hank's slicker was still tied on the saddle. He slipped it on and told Joe and Ann to start looking with the pickup while he searched with the horse. Joe took over driving and told Ann to watch for Hank as he would have

49.

to drive carefully to keep from running over
him if he was prone on the ground. After an hour
of searching, the storm broke for a bit and Ann
spotted Andy on a hill waving his hat furiously.
Joe hurried the old pickup to the sight. As
near as they could tell, Hank's horse had fallen
and the old man had been knocked unconscious.
Andy had found him face down in a draw with Ace
by his side. The old dog had tried to drag Hank
by the looks of the tracks. Ace must have sensed
that the draw they were in was filling with water
and threatened to drown his master. Hank started
to come to as Andy pulled him carefully out of
the water. He insisted on sitting up by the
time Joe and Ann arrived. They had tried to
keep him down in case of broken bones, but he
was adamant that he was o.k. They hadn't even
been able to get him to go to the doctor. He
was grateful that the kids had come looking for
him but after it was all over he insisted that
he would have been all right. Em contended that
he would have drowned and when he was really
ornery she would chastise Ann for saving his
life. All this was in fun, of course, as she
was so grateful for and loved her daughter-in-
law as if she were her own daughter. Of course,
to know Ann was to love her as she was totally
dedicated to Andy and the ranch.

The supper was delicious as usual and Hank
behaved himself pretty well. As usual he gave
Joe a bad time about getting his wife pregnant
at a time when the baby would be due in December.
Em was embarrassed and admonished the old man
by saying, "shut up Hank, that's not something
you decide by the calendar." He had just laughed
and said, "How is Joe going to get Nancy to the
doctor if we are in the middle of a blizzard?"
Nancy was no longer embarassed by anything Hank
would say. She was so excited about their family
that little disturbed her. Joe was just

as excited. Once again Ann came to everyone's
rescue. "We just figured that as many calves
as you have delivered you could deliver Nancy's
baby," she said. The old man was visibly
embarrassed at the thought of attending the birth
of a child. He sputtered and stammered and
finally said, "I'm not delivering a baby for
any one." Everyone laughed at his embarrassment
as Em added, "Well I have helped deliver many
babies and if necessary Ann and I will deliver
it."

With supper over the men retired to the
living room while Ann and Nancy helped Em clear
the table. The women got along exceptionally
well and loved to just visit over coffee. After
awhile they joined Hank, Andy, and Joe in the
living room to find that men had decided to drive
the yearling heifers to the railroad loading
pens and send them to Omaha to be sold. It was
either that or sell them on the ranch and then
load them on trucks to go to the eastern feedlots.
Rail freight was pretty cheap and the increase
in price that they would get in Omaha seemed
like the way to go.

Finally, the evening came to a close and
the young couples took their leave. Before they
left Ann sat on Hank's lap and placed a big kiss
on his leathery old cheek. He was embarrassed
as usual but loved ever minute of it. "Dang
females," he muttered as everyone laughed at
him.

As they left for hime, no one realized that
sleeping far away in Illinois a young man was
on his way to enter their lives.

Chapter 7

TEDDY'S LETTERS REACH BALTIMORE

The time in the hospital for Pat, Teddy's mom, had gone well. Frequent visits and phone calls from her husband Arlo had helped. Arlo was amazed at how clear his mind was after a month in alcohol rehab. He had made peace with himself as far as it being his fault that Teddy had left. He still knew it was mainly his fault but knew if Teddy was ever located he needed to have his health to be able to regain his sons faith. Arlo sorted through the mail each day, which came to him, and then he took the important articles to his wife. They were both looking forward to being released soon. As Arlo checked the mail, he noticed a beat up letter and picked it up. He recognized Teddy's handwriting and his hands shook as he tore the letter open. Tears streamed down his cheeks as he read his sons letter. What a kid he thought. He had aged way too fast just because his parents had been so stupid. Arlo hurried to the checkout desk with the letter in his hand. He wasn't supposed to go see Pat until five p.m. but had to see her sooner. Arlo found Amos Wright, the director of the rehab unit, in his office. Amos had taken a liking to Arlo and vise versa. Arlo's dad had died when he was young and although Amos was only bout five years older, he had almost became a substitute father to Arlo. "I got a letter form Teddy!" shouted Arlo as he entered the office. Amos jumped from his chair and hugged the elated man.

After showing the letter to Amos and asking him if he could leave early to take the news to Pat personally, Arlo rushed from the rehab center. He didn't wait for a bus to take him

to Pat's hospital. He hailed a taxi, as they
had requested that he not drive his car until
he was released from the rehab center.

Arlo rushed into Pat's room and totally
surprised her. He was hugging her and gave her
a kiss before she could say a thing. "Arlo why
are you so early?" she finally asked. He simply
showed her Teddy's letter. Pat read it not even
believing what she read. Finally the reality
sunk in and she couldn't control her elation.
After all these years she had started praying
again for Teddy's safety but down deep felt something had happened to him. She asked Arlo to
pray with her, which he gladly did. Afterward,
they looked the letter over and wondered at the
terrible condition it was in. It was written
in pencil, wrinkled, and stained. After they
discovered it was postmarked in Illinois, they
wondered how he was traveling. Shortly Pat's
nurse stepped into the room, "Excuse me, but
there is a phone call at the desk for either
Arlo or Pat Springer," she said. Arlo followed
her out as Pat clung to the letter. "Hello,"
said Arlo into the phone. "Is this Ted's dad?"
said the young voice on the other end of the
line. "Yes, this is Arlo Springer," he replied.
"This is Becky and I wanted to tell you I received
a letter from him today," she said. "We did
too," replied Arlo. "Was yours mailed in
Illinois?" he asked. "Yes," she replied. "I'll
read it to you if you want." she added. "Yes
please do," he said. After Becky had read the
letter to him he thanked her profusely and hurried
back to Pat's room. "That was Becky," he said
excitedly. "She got aletter also and Teddy told
her he was headed to Nebraska. Who would he
know in Nebraska?" Arlo asked. "I don't know,"
replied Pat, not thinking about the visit from
Ellen Jorden and the fact that Ann was living

in the sandhills. The hospital staff was elated
when they discovered that the Springers had heard
from their son. They quickly arranged for a
small celebration supper in Pat's room. They
ordered food from a restaurant and set up a table
lit only with candles. As they were enjoying
their supper, suddenly Pat exclaimed, "Ann
Jorden!" "What's that?" asked Arlo. "Ann Jorden,"
repeated Pat. "A couple months before Teddy left
Ellen Jorden visited me. She said Ann had
married a rancher and lived in the sandhills of
Nebraska. You remember how Teddy loved her.
I'll bet he is trying to find her," she told
her husband excitedly. "I'll try to call
immediately in the morning if they have phones,"
said Arlo. "I'll write Ann a letter," said Pat.
"I wonder if he can actually find them?" continued
Pat. "Well he has went a long ways already,"
said Arlo. "Sounds like he had a good teacher,
way better than his father ever was," he added.
"Don't hold it against yourself now," said Pat.
"We can't do that if we are to keep our health,"
she continued.

Meanwhile, in St. Louis, at the First
National Bank, senior vice president, Francis
Hooper, sat looking at a dirty stained piece of
paper on his huge desk. It had arrived a
couple of days ago and since then he had read
and reread it over and over. He turned it over
and looked at the rough map on the back and wondered again if it was a joke. He had told no
one of the letter and had sworn his secretary
to secrecy. The letter had been mailed near
a town where the three bank robbers had been
apprehended. If it was not a joke, why hadn't
the person just brought the money to the authorities. He finally called his head security
officer in and let him read it. He had kept
the letter quiet because if word leaked out it

would start a massive treasure hunt and the money may never be seen. After the officer read it and studied the map, Mr. Hooper said, "What do you think?" "Pretty strange," said the officer. "But what about this robbery hasn't been strange?" he added. They went on to discuss how it sure seemed to fit into the strange arrests that had been made. "I think you should take this map, locate that game warden that knew the area so well and check it out," said the banker. The officer agreed. They both agreed that the less said to the news media the better until the whole thing was checked out.

Meanwhile after traveling up the Mississippi until he found a bridge, Teddy had crossed over into Missouri.

Chapter 8

TEDDY AND TOBY CROSS MISSOURI

The two travelers were pleasantly surprised
when they reached Missouri. Teddy had thought
there would be lots of night traveling which
he had grown to despise. He had traveled so
much at night during the first half of his journey

that he knew he could do it but sure didn't want
to. Although, there were many open areas in
southern Missouri there were twice as many areas
with cover. He was no longer afraid to be seen
occasionally as no one seemed to be too curious
in this country. Although, they didn't wear
all buckskins like Teddy, they didn't wear much
better clothes and many even carried rifles.
He didn't realize he was fast approaching the
Mark Twain National Forest. Many farmers still
used horses and Teddy almost fit into the scene
in some of the small towns. He got pretty brave
until a county sheriff questioned him one afternoon after he had boldly walked through a small
town and evidently someone became suspicious
that he was a runaway. He had dismantled his
rifle and put it in his backpack. He told the
sheriff that he was from back east and spending
summer vacation hitch hiking from a relative
in southeastern Missouri to relatives near Kansas
City. He was sure the sheriff never bought his
story but he didn't hold himand he vowed to stay
away from towns after that. He didn't need to
go to town as game was plentiful and he had no
money anyway. He laughed as he thought that
he could have had one hundred fifty thousand
dollars to spend. People might have been a little
suspicious then, thought Teddy. He chuckled
again as he recalled seeing his reflection in
a plate glass window in the town he had passed

through. He had been amazed at the change.
He had grown at least an inch and put on at least
twenty pounds of solid muscle. His hair was
nearly to his shoulders and his skin was as dark
as Randy Silverfox. He supposed most people
mistook him for an Indian, which pleased him
very much as Randy was his idol. There were
several rivers to cross. Some of them he could
wade but a few he had to use a raft on. If he
had crossed the Mississippi where he thought
he did on the hand drawn map, he knew he wouldn't
reach the Missouri River until he was much further
Northwest. If he had it figured out right, he
could stay on the south side of the Missouri
River and follow it to Kansas City. He would
have to detour around Kansas City as someone
dressed like him in the late forties would look
pretty suspicious in the city.

It was after he reached Kansas City, that
Randy had told him to start watching for cattle
trucks with Nebraska license plates that were
heading west empty to load more feeder cattle
and bring them east. Randy had said he sould
reach that area towards fall when the cattle
would be moving out of the ranch country to the
feedyards. He knew nothing about crops but
thought it must be getting on into late August
or early September as the corn was beginning
to ripen and the nights were cool. He was making
good time now he thought. Some days he figured
he walked fifteen to twenty miles. There were
only two pairs of soles left in his pack for
his moccasins and he hoped they would last him
until he reached Milligan, Nebraska. Now and
then he found himself wondering what kind of
reception he would get there. He knew Ann though
and she would never turn him away.

Meanwhile, Ann had received word by mail
from Arlo and Pat Springer that Teddy had ran

away and they had reason to believe he was trying
to find her. They had explained that they had
tried to call but the condition of the phone
lines to the ranch were so bad that they never
had been able to get through. They also explained
the whole truth about why Teddy had left and
that they were attempting to straighten out their
lives. Ann was beside herself with worry. She
remembered Teddy as an eight-year old boy who
wouldn't survive a week by himself. Andy and
Joe both assured her that if he had made it to
Illinois he was doing a darn good job and the
Indian that Pat had mentioned in her letter
must have taught him well. They also convinced
Ann that there was no way of finding him between
Milligan and the Mississippi.

They were in the midst of fall calving and
very busy on the ranch. Ann and Hank rode most
of the time checking cows while Andy and Joe
hauled haystacks in with skidracks and two A
John Deere tractors that were as old as Andy.
They also finished up the large new shed in the
corral near the calving pasture. Hank had wanted
to build it for years. The third year he and
Em had owned the ranch an early winter storm
had nearly broke them by killing seventy head
of fall calves. From that day on they planted
groves of trees whenever they could and now all
of his mature cattle could weather a bad storm
with no problems. He had always worried about
his fall calves though and what they would do
if an early storm caught them again. The new
shed solved that problem. It was one hundred
twenty feet long and twenty feet wide. Joe and
Andy had left the area in the back with rails
just high enough for the calves to go under
but the cows couldn't enter. The cows had the
whole front part of the shed to stand in. Above
the back part where the calves would be, they
had made a hay mow and stored tons of bales of

hay which could be fed if a storm lasted several
days. Hank had put down a new well and windmill
near the center of the shed in front of it so
the cows could have access to water which was
critical in a storm.

Nancy was doing quite well in the late stages
of her pregnancy and all of her doctor reports
were good. The doctor told her that late November
was probably be when her baby was due. Around
two more months to wait seemed like an eternity.
She had finally quit working even part time for
Donna in the cafe and spent most of her time
getting ready for the baby.

Back in Illinois, the security officer and
game warden had returned to the place where the
bank robbers were arrested and spent two days
finding the area designated on Teddy's map.
Once they found the area they had no problem
locating the buried treasure. Now the story
of the letter and subsequent recovery of the
money was let out to the media and Teddy became
famous although he didn't know it.

No one else knew it either for a long time
until Hank heard about the money being recovered
on his new fangled radio. He was telling what
he heard to Andy, Ann, and Joe one afternoon
when Ann asked. "How did you say the letter
was signed?" "Why just yours truly Ted and Toby,"
said Hank. "You don't suppose that was Teddy
Springer?" she thought out loud. "His dad said
he had his dog, Toby, with him and he was in
that area. Did they say anythging about the
condition of the letter?" she asked Hank. "They
did say it was printed in pencil and looked like
it had seen some rough handling," he replied.
That night Ann sat down and wrote to Arlo and
Pat Springer telling them of the news Hank had
heard and asking them if they thought it could
have been Teddy. By this time, she was almost

sure it was and Hank had said the bank was offering a generous reward for whoever had foiled the robbers' plans.

September turned into October and Teddy worked his way up to the Missouri River and along it to Kansas City. From there he followed the river northwest into the southeast corner of Nebraska until he was about to Omaha. He was resting near a busy highway watching for stock trucks one day and realized that almost all of the vehicles had Nebraska license Plates. There were lots of trucks on the road but he had no way of knowing which ones were headed to where he wanted to go. If he could get to a station where they bought fuel, he thought he might do better. He continued up the river to the edge of Omaha. After finding a good camping place for the night, he left Toby with his pack and slipped into the city. Near the stockyards he located a station with two dozen or more cattle trucks parked in the parking lot. He slipped among them checking license plates and found they were nearly all Nebraska plates. As he was standing in the shadow of a truck, two men came from the cafe near the station. One of the men said, "Al, I'm going to rent a room for about a six hour nap then head to Grand Island to get another load of feeder cattle." That's my chance thought Teddy but how do I know which truck is his. Luck was on his side. The driver that had made the statement went to a truck in the line up, retrieved a small bag and headed for the motel near by. Teddy headed to the truck, memorized the license number, and looked to see that the end gate was tied open. Then he headed back to get Toby. He knew he had six hours but he wanted to be in the back of the truck well before the driver woke up. He and Toby returned to the station, crawled into the trailer and

60.

found it had been all cleaned out and four bales
of bedding were laying in the back. Teddy broke
one bale and spread it out in a small area near
the front of the trailer. He covered it with
his poncho and was soon sound asleep.

Chapter 9

A BUMPY DUSTY RIDE

Teddy jerked awake as the truck engine roared
to life. It was still dark when the driver pulled
out onto the road. Most of the highway was gravel
and some of it was quite bumpy. Dust boiled
into the back of the truck and covered Teddy
and Toby. "Well Toby this is easier than walking
but I would just as soon walk as sit in the dust,"
said Teddy. As they roared along, they covered
mile after mile. Teddy started thinking how
he would get out of the truck if it was daylight
when they arrieved in Grand Island. Maybe the
driver would stop to eat or something and he
could sneak out of the truck.

After about an hour and a half of driving
the sun came up and shined in the back of the
truck. Teddy felt the truck slowing down and
hoped they were not going to load cattle already.
He didn't think they could be in Grand Island
already. They pulled off at a small town and
the driver stepped out of the truck. There had
been another truck running ahead of them and
the two drivers approached each other as they
left their trucks. "Are you loading at Kearney
too?" the other driver asked the driver of the
truck Teddy was stowed away in. "I guess so,"
he replied as they went into the cafe. Teddy
quickly took out his home made map which was
getting to be in prety bad shape. He looked
at highway two from Grand Island to where he
thought Milligan was and there was no town of
Kearney. For the hundredth time he wished he
had a real map. The map he had made had only
the highways that he wanted to follow. Well
he had better try to get out at Grand Island
as he had no idea where Kearney was. after thirty

minutes, the drivers reappeared and they headed
down the highway. After what seemed like another
couple of hours, but probably wasn't, Teddy could
see they were approaching a larger town. How
to get out of the truck and hide in broad daylight
was a problem now. He would be pretty noticeable
in his bukskin garb in the middle of Grand Island.
Teddy gathered up his pack and he and Toby
stationed themselves near the end gate of the
truck waiting for a chance to jump out. The
truck slowed almost to a stop to turn a sharp
corner. With no cars coming from behind and
some tall grass in the ditch Teddy took a chance.
"Come on Toby," he called as he threw out his
pack and jumped out himself. Toby jumped out
and they hurried into the grass in the road ditch.
They lay in the grass awhile and then Teddy peeked
above the tall stems. They needed a place to
spend the rest of the day so they could walk
around Grand Island in the dark and find highway
two. He could see nothing close so he lay back
down in the grass. Another truck went by and

Teddy realized that from the cab he and Toby
could be seen even in the tall grass. They had
to do something. He peeked up again and saw
a farm wagon sitting in a field not too far away.
They waited until there was no traffic from either
direction and he and Toby made a run for it.
They reached the wagon and hid behind it while
Teddy caught his breath. Teddy then pulled himself up over the edge of the wagon and looked
in. It was empty so he tossed his pack and coat
in, then he helped Toby in and crawled in himself.
"I hope no farmer needs this wagon before dark,"
Teddy told Toby as they settled down for the
day.

It was a long day as riding in the truck
wasn't tiring and Teddy was restless. He cleaned
out his pack checked his dried meat and he and
Toby each ate a couple of pieces. Finally after

63.

dark, they crawled from the wagon and
headed north around Grand Island. For
the hundredth time he considered leaving
the fur coat bundle that Randy had made
him. He just couldn't do it though as
Randy worked hard making it and had told
him to keep it with him. They walked
rapidly north until they were well north
of the city lights. Finally they headed
west toward where his hand drawn map
showed they would find highway two.
After a long walk and crossing a well
traveled northbound highway, he saw cars
traveling northwest and figured that
had to be the highway, he wanted to
follow. He put several miles behind
him that night after his long rest.
There were quite a few farms along here
so he decided to travel at night for
awhile. The next few nights were unevent-
ful and the traffic was almost nonexistent
on the highway after ten o:clock. Teddy
covered many miles those nights as he
walked on the road and walked fast.
During the day, he was able to shoot
rabbits and squirrels with great success.
He and Toby ate well those days and enjoyed themselves tremendously. Finally
they passed Broken Bow, and the country
turned totally into sandhills. Teddy
was fascinated by the immensness of the
grasslands. They started traveling by
day and staying just out of sight of
the highway on the south side. Those
were good days and Teddy probably could
have made better time but he had unconsciously almost turned into the mountain
man that he looked like for by now even
though he had just turned thirteen he
looked much older. He had become pretty
self-efficient and maybe unconsciously

didn't want it to end too soon. Maybe
too it was the uncertainties of what
awaited him him in Milligan. He didn't
know Ann all that well and it had been
five years since he had seen her. Well
he had come a lot of miles and would
take whatever came when he found her.
He was sure he could handle a man's job
now as he had filled out his buckskin
clothes and was as strong as most
eighten year olds. It was well into
the fall now as the trees were changing
color and the crops that he did see were
nearly ripe. Game was plentiful even as he
worked more into the sandhills. His ammunition
was getting low but he wasn't worried as his
destination wasn't that far off. He and Toby
spent time investigating blowouts and even found
a couple of arrowheads left by the Indians of
long ago. That led him to think of Randy and
he wondered what was going on back at his camp
in the Appalachian Mountains.

Randy had become depressed after Teddy and
Toby left. He couldn't understand why. He had
been in the mountains alone aver a year and didn't
remember being so depressed. He hated to admit
he was lonely but supposed he was. He had enjoyed
teaching Teddy how to survive in the wilderness
and guessed he had hoped Teddy would decide to
stay with him. He knew it was no life for a
young boy though. At least Teddy had a destination in his mind and Randy found himself with
no destination at all. Well tomorrow was the
day for Eddie, Randy's brother, to bring his
mail out and put it in the hollow tree for Randy
to pick up. Eddie brought the mail out twice
a month, as Randy had left Eddies address for
anyone who might need to contact him. He hadn't
seen Eddie for two months so he decided to meet
him the next day. Randy was up early, since

he had no idea when Eddie would be there. He
only knew that he came on the second and fourth
Saturday of each month. They left it that way
in case Randy needed to see Eddie. Randy arrived
at the tree with a turkey he had shot on the
walk down the mountain. He cleaned the turkey
and started it roasting over a fire. He wondered
if Eddie would bring his two boys along. Randy
loved them and they thought Uncle Randy was special.
Around noon he heard Eddie's old Chevy car slowly
grinding up the mountain road. Randy was out
of sight of Eddie as he stepped from his car.
"How Chief," said Randy. "How Chief, to you
too," said Eddie. They had greeted each other
that way since they were very young. Allen and
Eric screamed with delight when they saw Randy.
They both jumped from the car and raced to him.
He held them one in each arm and laughed loudly
as they asked him a dozen questions. Finally
he said, "Will you guys have dinner with me?
I have a turkey roasting." Eddie said they had
all day as Mary and her sister had went shopping.
As they talked, Eddie said, "About gave up on
seeing you again Randy. It's been almost three
months since you met us here." "Well," replied
Randy, "I was a little depressed after my visitor
left." "Visitor?" said Eddie. "Yes, I found
a runaway boy and his dog sleeping in the mountains about a month ago. He was headed for
Nebraska. It took me a month to teach him to
live in the forest and make him some buckskins
and moccasins. His shoes were wore clean out
as he had walked from Baltimore," replied Randy.
"Was his name Teddy Springer and his dog Toby?"
asked Eddie. Randy was shocked, "How did you
know about him?" he asked. "Well, he became
a hero after he left here," laughed Eddie. He
went on to tell Randy about the bank robbers
and how they are sure Teddy was the one that
accosted them. Randy laughed and laughed at
the story. "I knew he was a special kid, but
had no idea he had that much forsight to come
66.

up with a plan like that," said Randy. "Well
if they ever locate him he will be pretty well
off for a young boy as the banker put a thousand
dollars in an escrow account for whoever foiled
the thieves," said Eddie. "Wow!" exclaimed Randy.
"I wonder where Teddy and Toby are now?" he continued. They talked for a long time, while the
boys played Indian scout in the trees. Eddie
asked Randy if he ever thought of going on to
college. He had been offered football scholar-
ships to several colleges when he graduated from
high school. He had been the states leading
passer his senior year but had chosen to serve
his country instead of going to school. Randy
told Eddie that he thought he was too old for
college or football. Eddie insisted that he
wasn't too old. He told him he was probably
in better condition now than when he got out
of high school.

Finally the turkey was done and they ate
dinner. The boys loved eating with their fingers
as Randy cut off chunks of turkey with his hunting
knife. Later when it was time for Eddie and
the boys to leave, Randy asked Eddie to type
two or three letters to some of the schools that
had recruited him out of high school. "I doubt
if any of them remember me," he told Eddie.
Eddie thought to himself, oh they will remember
you little brother. Randy went on to tell him
he would like to get a degree in something so
he could teach people how to live in harmony
with nature. After he saw how little Teddy knew
about conserving our natural resources, he knew
that the public needed some education about
natural resources.

As Eddie and the boys left, Randy knew his
days of isolation were numbered. Just like the
United States and the war he thought. You can
only look the other way so long, then you have
to try to do something.

67.

On the Evans ranch, it had been a very busy
late summer and fall. Since Hank had invested
in another skid rack to haul hay and put a winch
on his other old A John Deere, Andy and Joe had
made short work of hauling in the haystacks.
Hank and Ann spent many hours in the saddle
watching the fall calvers while Em and Nancy
canned jar after jar from Em's garden.

The yearling heifers had been brought in
and fifty head had been sorted off for replacement
cows. They were placed in a special corral that
would keep them from getting bred until the
following spring. They had drove the rest of
the heifers to the railroad corrals and loaded
them out to the Omaha stock yards for sale.
Hank had rode down on the same train and spent
three days seeing the heifers sold and returned
with the money by bus. The spring calvers had
been brought in. The calves were weaned and
watched closely for thirty days for sickness.
Light rains had kept the dust down in the corrals
so pneumonia was at a minimum and the calves
needed very little doctoring. After they weaned
the calves, the spring calving cows were turned
onto the hay meadows to utilize the good after-
grass that had came up after the hay was stacked.
About fourty-five days after weaning, the steers
were sorted off and driven to the railroad corrals
to be shipped to the stockyards in Grand Island.
It was tough drive with the short weaned steers.
It took Andy, Ann, Joe, Hank, and even Em to
get them started on the trail. Nancy followed
with Hank's old pickup. Ace erned his wages
also while driving the young steers. As soon
as they were off, the ranch and started good
they loaded Em's horse into the pick up and her
and Nancy returned to the ranch. It was about
a ten-mile drive to the corrals but it went well
once the calves figured out what was going on.
Em drove the pickup to the yards and picked up

Joe, Ann, and their horses first. Then Joe
returned to get Hank, Andy, and their horses
after the calves were loaded on the rail cars.
It was a bit crowded in the pickup on the way
home, as Ace had to ride beside Hank. Hank
wouldn't ride the train this time. He and Andy
would drive to Grand Island on sale day to watch
the calves sell. They wanted Joe to go as he
had a few of his calves in with them but he didn't
want to be that far from Nancy as the baby was
due in about thirty-days.

The three men arrived late with the horses
to find that the women had fixed a big supper
at Hank and Em's. It was a big day but sort
of a good feeling to have all of the market livestock off of the ranch before any bad weather
set in. As they ate supper, Ann asked Hank why
they sent the big cattle to Omaha and the spring
calves to Grand Island. Hank explained to her
that Grand Island seemed to have the best market
for spring calves. It seemed that farmers bought
them to background and if they didn't want to
finish them they would ship them on to the eastern
feed yards. From then on it was pretty routine
around the ranch.

Things were pretty routine for Teddy and
Toby too on these nice fall days. They traveled
almost as if they had no destination, but always
worked west with the highway in sight. Whenever
they spotted a town they slipped in at night
to see what town it was. Teddy had them all
written on his map so he had some idea of how
far it was to Milligan. Finally they arrived
at Thedford and that night when Teddy made camp
he figured they were about fifty miles from
Milligan. Days had passed swiftly by and it
was getting late into November. Nights were
pretty cold but Teddy didn't worry. He could
usually find cow chips or wood for fire and was
very careful as the sandhill grass was mature

and had frozen and would burn easy. Two days
later found his camp about thirty miles east
of Milligan. He had still been fortunate enough
to shoot Jack rabbits and had shot a couple of
ducks off of a sandhill pond.

Chapter 10

ANIMAL INSTINCT AND A WOMEN'S INTUITION

Toby woke Teddy up well before daylight, which
was unusual. "What's the matter Toby?" asked
Teddy as the dog kept whining and trying to get
Teddy to break camp. Teddy wasn't in any hurry
but Toby just kept agitating him until they were
on their way.

When they did take off instead of roaming
around and hunting, the dog just kept trotting
far ahead and looking back at Teddy. "Wish you
could talk," puffed Teddy as he followed the
dog. About noon they came upon a single cotton-
wood tree that had been blown over by a summer
south wind. Apparently, it was the only tree
in that pasture and the cattle had stood around
it so much that its stability had been weakened.
There was a large hole where it had been uprooted.
The hole had been enlarged by an old herd bull
that was either challenging another bull or trying
to keep the flies off his back by pawing and
throwing sand . Toby stopped at the tree and
let Teddy catch up. "Well do we at least get
a rest for lunch?" asked Teddy. He unwrapped
some cold duck meat from the night before. The
dog refused the meat and kept looking north and
sniffing the breeze. It was a warm day with
a soft southern breeze. Suddenly Teddy noticed
that the breeze had died completely down. Within
a few minutes, the breeze began to blow again
only now it was from the north and was much
cooler. Teddy picked up his pack and headed
west after a short break. Toby refused to leave
the tree. "What's the matter Toby?" asked Teddy
when he wouldn't even follow when he called.
Now the wind had picked up and Teddy noticed
how cool it was. Clouds were starting to roll
in and the air felt damp. Teddy started to become

concerned. "Is there a storm coming?" Teddy
asked his dog. All the sudden he was sure there
was. He remembered Randy telling him animals
had a sixth sense about things like that. "You
think we should use this old tree for protection
don't you," he said to Toby.

Teddy went to work in a hurry. He gathered
some large branches to cover the hole behind the
tree roots after he had used the small army shovel
to clean out the bottom of the hole. After he
had large branches over the hole, he used his
hatchet to cut some branches off that had the
dried leaves stuck to them like they do when a
tree us uprooted in the summer. He had to reach
high to get these as the cattle had eaten all
of the leaves from the low branches. Teddy lay
these over the large branches to seal up the holes.
The wind had picked up considerable now and threatened to blow the leafy branches off. Teddy
hurriedly grabbed some more large branches to
put on top to hold the roof on. By this time,
it was spitting snow and Teddy took time to look
north into the wind. What he saw sent a lump
to his throat. There was a wall of white sweeping
across the prairie towards him. Toby had been
right, it was a blizzard. He grabbed his pack
and fur coat, and shoved them into the dugout.
Suddenly he remembered his hatchet. He had left
it on the tree. He scrambled to get it and was
just back to the small hole entrance he had left
when the storm hit. It took his breath away as
he slid into the hole with Toby right behind him.
He turned to pull some branches over the hole
as snow was already sifting in. Teddy pulled
his poncho from the pack and put it up against
the north side of the hole. Then he pulled it
up over his head and tucked it into the branches
in case snow sifted through his make shift roof.
By now, the wind was howling so loud it hurt
Teddy's ears. "I guess I owe you my life again,"
he said as he hugged the dog. Toby finally laid

down. He had been on edge all day and evidently felt he had done all he could. "Well," said Teddy. "Randy, wherever you are, thanks again. I"ll never be able to repay you for what hou have done for me." He settled down for what was going to be a long prairie blizzard that would dump two feet of snow in the sandhills.

That same morning on the Evans ranch Joe found Hank, Andy, Ann, and Ace gathered in the center of the yard when he came to work. Andy and Hank were in earnest conversation. When Joe drove up he asked what was going on and Andy replied, "Dad and Ace think there is a storm coming." "We don't think there is a storm coming, we know there is a storm coming," said the old rancher. "Seems pretty nice out to me," said Joe. "That don't mean a thing," replied Hank. Andy spoke up, "Dad's arthritis and Ace have been predicting weather pretty accurate for years and I don't question them any more than I do Ann when she says something is wrong."

"Well whats the plan then?" asked Joe. "Ann and Dad are going to saddle up and go round up the spring calving cows in the meadow," said Andy. He went on to explain that they would drive them to the shelter belt in the northwest corner of the hay meadow. This was the grove Hank and Em had planted the spring after the winter that had nearly cost them the ranch. They had planted five rows of cedar trees in an L shape in the corner of the meadow. Later they had put a stack yard on each leg of the L and they also added two more rows of trees about one hundred yards to the south of the first grove. Hank had put a windmill and tank in the center of the L and after thirty-five years it was a terribly good grove of trees.

"While they run the spring calvers to the

73.

trees you and I better crank up our hay hauling
rigs and each load a stack. We will hay between
the trees so the cows will stay there. While
we pitch off the hay, Ann and Dad will round up
the fall calvers and bring them into the new shed.
"We probably should scatter a couple of stacks
in that corral also," said Andy. Hank and Ann
had already hustled off to get their horses and
Joe, feeling the urgency now ran towards his A
John Deere and was checking the oil as Andy was
finishing his instructions. They both heard the
screen door slam and looked up to see Em coming
from the house. She had her arms full of items
and she headed directly to the pickup. "Where
are you going Mom?" asked Andy. "If there is
a storm coming and you are all running around
chasing cows, I'm going to be with Nancy. All
we need is for a storm to hit and have her home
alone. Her time is too close for that. As soon
as Joe is done here and comes home, I'll be back,"
replied Em in her no nonsense tone of voice as
she started to get in the ranch pickup. "Take
my car Em in case we need the pickup here," called
Joe. "Suits me fine," said Em. "I can hardly
drive that old pickup anymore anyway," she continued. She was soon chugging out of the yard
in Joe's faithful old Ford car. Joe hurried to
put fuel in his tractor and hook to the skidrack.

It seemed nothing would go right because
he was in a hurry. First the stack cable wrapped
around a skidrack wheel and he had trouble getting
it out. He didn't clean the hay out good enough
from around the stack and the cable started to
slide up and would either tip the stack over or
leave two ton of hay on the ground. He had to
release the winch and reset the cable. It looked
like Andy almost had his stack on already before
Joe was ready to winch the second time. He
finally got loaded and hitched on the skidrack.
He wasn't far behind when they pulled the two
stacks up to the shelter belt. The cows were
already starting to drift in, so they knew Hank,

Ace, and Ann were on the job. Andy waved Joe
to the east end of the shelter belt while he
went to the west side. They wouldn't be able
to tie the steering wheels and let the tractors
go in these tight quarters so they would have
to crawl up the stack pitch off a bunch of hay
then slide down and move the tractors. Hank
and Ann couldn't take time to drive for them
because they had to get the fall calving cows
and calves rounded up and into the corral. Joe
could see how strange the cows were acting as
he pitched as fast as he possibly could. They
kept two pitchforks with each outfit so they
could climb up the five ton stacks sort of like
mountain climbing. It took a fair amount of
time to unload five tons of hay but both Andy
and Joe were in good shape and worked hard.
Their outfits were almost together when they
pitched off the last hay. Andy ran over and
said, "Let's go load two more Joe and put them
in the corral for the fall calver." Cows were
gathered around now so Andy continued out of
the shelter belt the way Joe had come in and
Joe went the opposite direction. They had to
go slow as the cows paid very little attention
to the tractors. Finally clear of the cattle,
they headed back to reload.

Hank and Ann hit the calving pasture with
Ace right behind them. "Hunt calves Ace," shouted
Hank and the old dog took off for the hills at
a bpe. "He will find any calves hidden out by
their mothers Ann. Let's start pushing cows
and calves towards the ranch. If you have an
old cow that insists on turning back. let her
go. Chances are she has her calf hidden and
Ace will bring her later," said Hank. Ann was
alreday riding off to do the job before them.
They rode hard and Ann felt the wind go calm
and then start blowing out of the north. When
she topped the hill just west of the ranch with

about a hundred cows and calves, Hank was coming
in from the north with a larger herd of his own.
She had let a half dozen heard quitters turn
back and told Hank so when they got close enough
to talk. "That's alright, Ace will bring them,"
said Hank. Joe and Andy were already in the
large corral pitching hay. Ann and Hank tied
their horses and each crawled on a tractor to
move them for the men so they dicn't have to
get off the stack. While they were pitching
hay, Ace topped the hill west of the ranch with
six cows and calves. As soon as they were in
the corral, Hank crawled from his tractor, went
to the gate, pointed north and said, "More Ace."
The old dog was gone in a flash. They were just
pulling the tractors out of the corral when
Ace appeared from the north with four more pair.
 When they were in the corral, Hank shut the
gate and the wind was picking up noticeably
by now. The air felt damp.

    Ann and Hank took their horses to the barn.
They were well lathered up from the hard ride
so they unsaddled them, fed them, and rubbed
them down. They were still working on them when
Joe and Andy entered the barn. "Boy, you can
feel it now in the wind," said Andy as the plopped
down on the hay. Ace was already laying down
still panting. Everyone had huge workout and
Ace, Andy, and Joe were about spent. "You boys
pitched ten ton of hay each quicker than it's
ever been done before I bet," said Hank. "man
I feel it too," said Joe as he scratched Ace's
ears. "By the way Dad, Mom went to be with Nancy
until Joe gets home," said Andy. "I saw Joe's
car tearing through the meadow ten miles an hour
when we were rounding up the spring calvers and
figured Em wouldn't leave Nancy there alone,"
said Hank. Then he asked, "What's left to do
now Andy?" "Just crank up the loader tractor
and push hay up to the feed racks for the

76.

replacement heifers and the weaned heifers,"
said Andy. Well we can handle that. Joe you
head for home and send Em back," replied Hank.
"It's starting to snow pretty good," said Joe
as he opened the barn door. "If you guys don't
need me, I'll ride over so I can drive Em home.
You know how she gets mad at the pickup," said
Ann. "Go," said Hank. The urgency in the old
mans voice was all Ann needed and she ran out
to hop in the pickup with Joe. As they drove,
the three miles to Joe's house Ann said, "Far
cry from living in Philadelphia isn't it Joe?"
he laughed and replied, "Yes, but you know I
wouldn't trade this life for any I have
experienced yet." Me either, I love it out here,"
replied his sister. The snow was getting thicker
and thicker now and when they reached Joe and
Nancy's house, Ann hurried Em into the pickup
and they headed home. "Call as soon as you get
there. I think the phone lines are still up
between here and there!" shouted Joe as they
drove off. Nancy hugged Joe a long time when
he got into the house from feeding his saddle
horse in the small barn west of the house. "I'm
scared," she said. "Don't be scared, we are
safe here at home," replied Joe. "I hope Ann
and Em get home safe," said Nancy as she looked
out. You could hardly see the small horse barn
Andy and Joe had built. It wasn't long and the
phone jangled on the wall. "Hello," said Joe
as he picked it up. "This is Em Joe. We made
it alright. Hank and Andy just finished feeding
and everyone is in the house," she said. "Good,"
said Joe. "I hope the lines hold," he started
to say but it was no use the rickety old line
had already went down. "Well at least we know
they are all in the house and the livestock is
situated for a storm," he said as he hung up
the useless phone. By now you couldn't even
see the small barn or the wood shed that was
only twenty feet from the house. The roar of

the wind was high pitched and had an erie sound.
"Did you carry all that wood in?" asked Joe.
When he noticed the wood box was piled high plus
a large stack on the floor. "No, Em did all
that she wouldn"t let me lift a stick," laughed
Nancy. Joe just shook his head and laughed.

Thirty odd miles to the east Teddy hugged
Toby close as the wind roared over their heads.
It was surprisingly warm in their cave. Finally
they both drifted off to sleep. Teddy's last
thought before sleep overcame him was that Randy
had said don't worry about what you can't control.
Well he sure couldn't control the wind so he
would just wait it out.

At the ranch, Em had slammed the receiver
down on the phone when it went dead and said,
"Danged modern inconveniences. They work great
when the weather is nice and you don't need them
but when it gets bad and you need them they don't
work. Just watch, the fabulous electricity will
go off too!" It was no more than out of her
mouth and the power blinked off and on again.
"See there , what did I tell you Hank?" she
exclaimed. Hank just laughed and replied, "Now
Emmy settle down we still have our coal oil lamps
and besides remember how romantical we used to
get when it stormed?" "Don't romantical me you
old coot," Em exclaimed. Hank laughed loudly
as he patted Ace on the head. "I guess we are
getting old aren't we Ace," he said. "Well we
got a fine son out of that romance Em," he
continued. "Yes and I thank the Good Lord for
that every night. I also thank him for sending
Joe and Ann to us," she said as she prepared
the lamp for the inevitable time when the power
would fail. It was early yet but the storm was
so bad that it was almost dark in the house.
"What a pair, you would never know they was city
raised. Why Joe pitched ten ton of hay as fast
78.

as Andy and that sister of his amazes me every
time I see her ride. She rides just like you
did when you were that age," said Hank. "What
do you mean rides like I did? Are you saying
I'm over the hill Hank Evans?" exclaimed Em.
Hank knew he was in trouble now. "O.K., O.K.,
I mean she rides just like you do," he hurriedly
explained. With that, the power failed and Em
lit the lamp with the matches she was holding
in her hand for that very purpose. She put her
arm around Hanks shoulder and said, "We sure
have been blessed Hank. I wouldn't trade all
the years we have spent on this ranch for anything
in the world."

Three miles to the east at Joe and Nancy's,
the power failed also. Joe helped Nancy light
a lamp and finish doing dinner or supper dishes,
as they had eaten so late they just combined
both meals. He rubbed the frost off the window
and looked out for the twentieth time. "Sure
glad I'm not camped out on the prairie in this
storm," he commented. "How would you ever survive
out there?" asked Naancy. "I don't know what
you would do without protection," replied Joe.
It was early when they retired. Joe ached all
over after pitching all of that hay and Nancy
rubbed his sore shoulders before they blew out
the lamp. About three hours later, Nancy awoke
with a start. Had she felt a pain or was it
a dream. She lay quietly so as to not dusturb
Joe. She couldn't see the clock but about fifteen
or twenty minutes later she felt another sharp
 pain. At first she almost panicked. Settle
down, she told herself. don't make things worse
by getting scared, she thought. She shook Joe
lightly, "Joe, Joe wake up," she said. "What's
wrong Nan?" he asked. "I've had a couple of
pains now," she said. Joe just lay there like
her words didn't register. "What!" he shouted
all of the sudden. "Oh no, what will we do now?"

he said as he jumped out of bed and started to
dress. "I wish Em was here now," continued Joe.
"Do you think her and Ann can get here in this
storm?" asked Nancy. Trying not to show the
fear she felt inside. "I'll have to try to bring
them,"said Joe as he dressed and began to bundle
up. "What if you get lost in this storm?" cried
Nancy, as she doubled up in pain. She had lit
a lamp and carried it to the kitchen where Joe
was putting on all the overcoats he could find.
"I won't get lost as the horses can go back and
forth between here and the ranch blindfolded,"
he said. "I am worried about Em making the trip
over here in the storm and the time it is going
to take for me to get them," he continued. Nancy
hugged him and told him to be careful as he pushed
out into the blinding blizzard.

Over at Ann and Andy's about an hour before
Nancy even felt the first pain, Ann sat straight
up in bed. "Andy, Andy," she shouted. Andy
fought awake, "What?" he grumbled. He was wore
to a frazzle just like Joe. "Something is wrong,
we have to get to Joe and Nan," she cried already
starting to dress in the dark room. "Are you
sure?" asked Andy as he lit the lamp. "Maybe
your just excited from the hard day," he continued. "No we have to go," Ann insisted. Andy
knew there was no use arguing with his wife so
he hurriedly started to dress. Ten minutes later
found them pushing intoHank and Em's house calling
out to the old couple. "Mom, Dad," said Andy.
"Oh boy, can't even get any peace and quiet in
a blizzard anymore," muttered Hank as Em fumbled
to light a lamp. "What is it Andy?" asked Em.
"Ann says we have to get to Joe and Nancy because
something is wrong. We just wanted to let you
know we were going," said Andy. "I should hope
to say," said Em as she started to dress. "What
are you doing Mom?" asked Andy. "Your mother
is going with you. That's what she's doing,"
said Hank as he pulled the covers up

80.

over his head. "It's terrible out there Mom,"
said Andy and Ann at the same time. "Your not
telling me anything I don't know," said Em.
"I been in a lot more blizzards than you two
put together." "You guys have fun out there.
I'll stay her with Ace and hold down the ranch,"
came Hank's muffled voice from under the covers.
Ace was nervous with the goings on. Hank finally
sat up and comforted his old dog, "It's o.k.
Ace," he said. Andy had headed for the barn
to saddle horses. Em was finally bundled up
and had her doctor book and other supplies
securely tied in a bag over her shoulder. "Good
luck delivering that baby," Hank said as they
started out of the door. They both stopped in
their tracks. "How do you know thats what the
problem is?" asked Ann. "Well what else would
it be Annie? Them babies always come at the
most inconvenient time they can. Besides, I
know you pretty good and even if you do drive
me crazy once in awhile, we all know I wouldn't
be here it it wasn't for your uncanny ability
to foresee trouble," said Hank. Ann turned back
went to the old rancher and gave him a big kiss
on the head. He was embarrassed as usual but
loved every bit of it. "Cut the mushy stuff
Ann. We have a baby to deliver," said Em as
Andy shouted through the storm. They went out
and Andy helped the women on as their extra
clothes made it impossible to mount up alone.
You could hardly breath out in the wind. It
was almost like a vacuum. Andy tied Ann and Em's
horses together with a lariet rope then wrapped
it around his saddle horn. He lined his horse
out towards Joe's and then just hunkered down
to brave the storm. They had gotten quite a
head start on Joe as Ann had rousted them out
much quicker than Nancy had Joe. They forced
their way through the storm for what seemed like
two hours when in fact it had been less that half
that. All of the sudden, Andy's horse ran head

on into something. He brushed the frozen ice
from his eyelids and saw Joe in front of him.
They rode close and Joe shouted, "What in sam
hill are you doing?" "Your sister said we needed
to get over here right away so here we are!"
shouted Andy after he unwrapped his scarf from
his face. "Let's go," said Joe as he turned
around. Fifteen minutes later found them at
Joe's front door. Joe and Andy helped Ann and
Em off and practically carried them into the
house. Nancy was stunned when they walked in
looking like ghosts. "How in the world did you
get here so quick?" she asked as she bent over
in pain. "Never you mind that young lady," said
Em. "Just get in that bedroom and lay down while
Ann and I get these coats off. Andy and Joe
went to take care of the horses as quickly as
possible. The small barn was pretty crowded
but the old ranch horses were so glad to be out
of the storm that they behaved quite well. Within
minutes the men were back in the house. Em and
Ann were preparing for the new arrival in a business like manner. Joe stuck his head in the
bedroom only to have Em tell him to get some
water heating and leave them to do the women's
work. With that, he sat a kettle on the stove
stoking the fire more while preparing himself
for a two or three hour wait.

Chapter 11

THE NEW ARRIVAL

Em and An prepared for the ordeal ahead
with a lot less confidence than they showed.
After getting Nancy settled on the bed with a
plastic table cloth covered with a sheet under
her, Em timed the contractions. They were only
minutes apart now so she checked the progress
and found the baby's head easily touched. "Keep
up the good work Nancy. This isn't going to
take long," she said. Nancy was sweating profusely mostly from the pain. She pushed each
time there was a contraction and before long
Em was holding a baby boy in her hands. "It's
a boy," Ann said to Nancy quietly as Em directed
her to tie the cord off and where to cut it.
All the while, Em was suctioning mucus from the
Baby's nostrils and mouth with a small suction
device. She had prepared herself, in case this
very thing happened when she found out Nancy
would deliver in the winter. Em wrapped the
baby in clean dry towels and handed him to Ann.
"Watch him closely to make sure he keeps breathing
all right and you had better tell Joe and Andy,"
she said. Ann took a moment to marvel at the
miracle in her arms. Meanwhile, Em was telling
Nancy to push a few time more to help remove
everything that needed to be shed along with
the baby. Nancy pushed several times and then
said, "This is almost as hard as having another
baby." Em and Ann's eyes met instantly. Em
immediately checked Nancy again and said, "Your
right girl, I can feel another head. Didn't
the doctor ever mention two heartbeats?" "Only
once, a long time ago, I had forgotten all about
it, as he never mentioned it again," said Nan
as she pushed again. Em was really worried now.
She had heard so many times of the second of

a set of twins being still born or having brain
damage for lack of oxygen. "Lord let this baby
be all right," she whispered as Nancy worked hard
to deliver it. After a few tense moments, Em
stood holding a small baby girl that seemed
ever bit as responsive as the boy. "She's o.k.,
she's o.k." whispered Ann to Nancy as she kissed
her on the forehead. The girl was crying loudly
already and Joe and Andy grinned broadly at one
another. Joe went to the door and asked, "is
everything o.k.?" Ann opened the door a crack
and said "Everything is fine." "Is it a boy or
girl?" asked Joe. "Yes," said Ann as she closed
the door. "As soon as we are ready you can
come in," said Ann through the door. "What kind
of answer is that?" said Joe to Andy who was
standing right behind him. "I still don't know
if it's a boy or girl. That wife of yours is
nuts," he continued. "It's your fault, she's
your sister," said Andy as he shook his head.

Em and Ann cleaned Nancy up with the water
Joe had heated. They put clean dry bed clothes
on the bed and settled Nancy on the bed and put
a baby in each arm. "O.K. Dad, you can come in,"
said Ann as she opened the door. Joe rushed
to the door and froze in his tracks when he saw
Nancy with the twins. Andy was right behind him
but couldn't see as Joe was stuck in the door.
He gave Joe a shove and said, "Come on man let,"
and he froze in mid sentence as he saw the babies.
"Twins!" Joe finally blurted out. The women were
laughing in spite of their weariness at the stunned
looks on the two mens faces. Both men started
to talk at once. Neither one said anything that
made any sense. Finally, Ann interrupted with,
"What will you name them Nancy?" "That's the
easy part Ann. Let me introduce you to Annie
and Andy Jorden." Ann squealed in delight and
Andy smiled from ear to ear.

Em was soon back in control. "Shoo, shoo, you guys get out of here we have to see if these babies are ready to eat," she said. Andy and Joe retreated to the kitchen where Andy shook Joe's hand vigorously. "Congratulations old boy, I can't wait to tell Dad," he said. Joe replied, "What will Hank say when he finds out?" "I bet he says, doubled your herd the first year," laughed Andy. They poured more coffee, which they didn't need, and sat at the table. After a time, Ann and Em emerged grom the bedroom. They both looked worse for the wear. "Well they are all asleep," said Ann as she sat on Andy's lap. "Aren't they beautiful Andy?" she added. "Yes, they are beautiful," said Andy. "You and Em look terrible though. You better have some coffee and try to get some rest," he added. "Has the storm subsided any?" asked Em. No one had paid any attention to the storm so Joe went to the door and peeked out. "Still pretty bad," he said as he closed the door. "I can't believe Dr. Manly didn't know she was going to have twins. Wait until I see him." said Em. "I can't believe any of this," said Joe. "Well you will believe it by the time you get those two raised," laughed Andy.

It was nearly five a.m. by that time and Em said, "Oh my Ann we didn't write down what time they were born." They finally decided Andy was born at three-thirty and Annie was about fifteen minutes later. They visited for a bit and then Andy said, "I better get back to the ranch so Dad don't decide to go check cows or something." Ann replied, "You sit down Andy and I'll whip up some breakfastand then you can head back. While I get some breakfast, talk Em into laying down on the couch for awhile. She has to be beat." "I'm fine," insisted Em, but her weariness was beginning to show through.

After they had eaten pancakes, bacon, and
eggs, Joe and Andy left the house and headed
for the barn. The women had decided they could
manage so Joe was going to go with Andy to the
ranch and check things out. The storm had abated
a little but very little as they saddled and
headed to the ranch.

Far to the east, Teddy pushed through the
snow over the entrance of his cave. The snow
had drifted high over the top of the tree roots.
Luckily, the entrance was off to the east side
a bit so only about a foot of snow as over it.
His legs were stiff and sore from being cramped
up so long. When he pushed his head out, he
could at least stretch out his legs. It was
still storming furiously but he remained that
way for some time just to rest his cramped legs.
It had been plenty warm in the hole just as Randy
had told him. He remembered Randy telling of
two men surviving a blizzard by burying themselves
in the snow. Finally he slid back down into
the cramped space and dug out some well aged
dried meat. "We just as well eat tree branches
Toby," he said as they both chewed on a piece
of meat.

Joe and Andy approached the ranch through
a noticeably weaking storm. True to their
thinking Hank and Ace were crossing the yard
towards the barn when they rode into the the
yard. Hank shouted as soon as he saw them, "everything go o.k.?" he asked. "You bet," called
Andy. "Tell him Joe," he added. "Nancy had
twins Hank, a boy and a girl," said Joe as the
rode up. The old rancher let out a warwhoop
that startled both horses and Ace. "Well I'll
be doubled your herd in one year," said the old
man as Andy winked at Joe. They visited a bit
and planned how thy would check the cattle.

At Joe's house Em, Ann, and Nancy sat staring

at the two babies. "How will I ever thank you
two," said Nancy. "No need to thank anyone,
just the sight of two healthy babies is the only
thank you anyone needs," replied Em. "Oh naming
little Annie after me was more thank you than
I deserve," said Ann. "Hope the men made it
all right," she added. "They will be fine,"
said Em. "I wish I could have seen the look
on Hanks face when they told him," replied Ann.

By evening the storm had wound down. It
cleared just about sundown as the three tired
ranchers rode back to the house. The cattle
had faired really well with all of the preparation
and they had found no dead cattle. Hank and
Andy dismounted in front of the barn. "Bet Dad
is headed home," said Hank as he winked at Andy.
Joe grinned and nodded as he turned his tired
horse towards home.

Just before dark Teddy poked his head out
and saw that the storm was over. "Tomorrow we
head out Toby. It can't be that much further
and I'll bet game will be hard to find after
this storm," he said as he scratched Toby's ears.
They tried to make themselves comfortable for
one more night in their cave as the clearing
of the sky would mean a cold night tonight.
Teddy was pretty sure he would have to spend
one more night out before he reached Milligan,
but he hadn't taken into consideration walking
in the snow. He did have a half dozen dry matches
left and a half dozen pieces of dried meat even
though it was pretty bad. Well he had came
this far the last few miles weren't going to
stop him now.

Chapter 12

A TOUGH LAST THIRTY MILES

Teddy and Toby dug out the following morning
to a bright sunshiny November day. Teddy was
stiff and sore from sitting out the blizzard.
"Wasn't much Toby but it and you saved our lives,"
said Teddy as he looked back at the haven they
had used for shelter. It didn't take long to
find out that it was going to be tough walking
with all the snow on the ground. Teddy was
remembering Randy's snow shoes hanging in the
cabin. Sure wish I had snow shoes he thought
as he sunk in to his knees time and time again.
Where the drifts were blown in it was hard enough
to walk on top but every where else he broke
through. By the time the sun was overhead, the
snow was softer yet as it was well over thirty-
two degrees. Teddy shed his fur coat and hat
and wrapped them up in a bundle again. Guess
I won't even consider leaving them behind again
thought Teddy. It would have been mighty cold
through the blizzard without them and he wasn't
there yet. By three o:clock, he was soaking
wet almost to the waist and almost plumb wore
out. He didn't know how far he had came but
he knew it wasn't nearly as far as he wanted
to be. If he would have only thought to work
his way to the highway, someone would have gladly
given him a ride, if it was open yet. Staying
away from people was so deeply engrained in his
mind by now that the thought didn't even cross
his mind. Finally just before dark, he came
upon an old wooden windmill tower that had fallen
down and was just a pile of boards. He chopped
and broke up boards until he had a good pile.
They were wet on the outsiide but the snow hadn't
soaked in too far. He took one of the four by
for legs and chopped the damp outside wood off.

Then he made a pile of dry wood chips to try
to start a fire. When he unwrapped his matches,
there were six left. His hands were cold and
his wet legs left him chilled all over. The
third match finally lit the pile of wood chips.
He had underestimated the dampness of the boards
and his chip pile burned out before he could get
a board to burn. He hurriedly chipped up another
pile of wood chips. This time he split up some
of the boards into smaller pieces so when his
second too last match finally lit the wood chips,
he fed the splintered boards into the small blaze.
It was totally dark before the fire finally blazed
up and Teddy could feel the heat. He shook something fierce when he started to warm up. He
stayed up well into the night stoking the fire
and trying to warm up and dry out. It was difficult with all the snow covering but he finally
managed to get warmed up enough and dry enough
to roll up in his poncho and sleep. He had put
some of the larger pieces of wood on the fire
before he slept but even with that he was awake
in a couple of hours and cold again. He restoked
the fire and fell asleep again.

The next time he woke up the eastern skyline
was beginning to show. He built the fire up
one more time, melted some snow in his cooking
pot and threw the last scraps of dried meat into
it. After they boiled awhile, he cooled it some
and drank the warm broth. It was almost tasteless
but the warm water helped him warm up good.
It had gotten pretty darn cold during the night
as the snow was crusted pretty hard. Teddy fished
the pieces of meat out of the pot and shared
them with Toby. "Let's go old boy," said Teddy
as he packed up and headed out. They covered
ground pretty well until about ten o:clock when
the crust got soft and he started to break through
again. He struggled another long day and was
still seven or eight miles from Milligan when
it got dark. All he could find was a pile of

wet hay to try to burn. It was only about a
large pitch fork full that had fallen off a stack
as it was hauled in. The hay was laying in a
spot where the snow had blown off or it would
have been covered up. Teddy dug into the hay
and finally found a little dry in the middle.
He pulled out his one last match and for an instant didn't think the hay was going to light.
It finally did and Teddy fed the wet hay into
the blaze slowly so it wouldn't go out. He got
more smoke than heat from the wet hay and was
far from dry or warm when it was gone. He wrapped
up in his poncho and shivered through the worst
night of his life. Luckily it didn't get as
cold as the night before or he would have been
in bad shape.

It was hard to make his legs work the next
morning, but he was up at day break walking west.
With hardly any crust on the snow he was wetter
than ever by midmorning. By late afternoon,
he could feel his strength starting to give out.
At dark he could see the lights of a town. He
knew he had to make it tonight. Another cold
night and he might not get up. It was after
ten when he struggled down main street. When
he passed the post office he could see the words
by the street light. "Milligan, Nebraska," he
said outloud. "Well Toby we finally made it
to Milligan. Now what do we do old boy?" Maybe
we should find a policeman and let him put us
in jail. he thought. He didn't realize that
there wasn't even a policeman in Milligan or
even a jail for that matter.

Teddy walked on down the sidewalk and was
by the alley of Donna's Diner when a car
approached. He and Toby ducked into the alley
and ran behind the diner. "Don't know what we
are running for if we want to get caught," Teddy
said to Toby. As they stood behind the diner,

he heard a thump, thump in the dark. He walked
towards the sound and found the old storm door
on the rear of the diner banging in the stiff
wind. Must have forgot to lock the outside door
thought Teddy. He reached in for no reason and
tried the inside door. To his surprise, it opened
easily. Careless people left their door unlocked
he thought as the warm air drifted out to meet
him. It was just too tempting to resist. He
stepped inside with Toby an his heels. Maybe
I'll just warm up a little he thought as he
located the source of heat. Donna had a small
oil stove in the kitchen where Teddy was. He
sat down on the floor in front of the heater.
Nothing ever felt so good that he could remember
of in his entire life. He no more than started
to warm up and he was sound asleep with Toby
curled up beside him.

Bright and early the next morning Donna
unlocked the front door and entered the diner.
She flipped on the light, turned up the large
oil heater in the dining room and headed to the
kitchen to turn up the kiitchen heater. She
turned on the light and froze in mid stride
as she saw the sight before her. Toby had heard
her come in but evidently figured she was no
danger to Teddy as he just sat up and looked
at her.

"Well I'll be," she said. With that, Teddy
sat straight up. "I'm, I'm sorry maam," he
stammered. "I didn't mean to stay, I just wanted
to warm up," he continued. "It's o.k.," said
Donna. "Anyone is welcome here in an emergency,"
she added. "Where did you come from young man?"
she asked. "Baltimore," said Teddy. "Teddy
Springer and Toby!" exclaimed Donna. "You know
me?" asked Teddy in amazement. "I should say
so. Everyone has been on the look out for you
for months, ever since your folks and Ann Evans
figured out that you might be headed this way,"

said Donna. About that time Donna heard Sally
Barnes enter the cafe. Sally had taken over
Nancy's job after she quit to have her babies.
"Come here," Donna called as she winked at Teddy.
Sally came through the door and nearly fainted
when she saw the sight before her. Teddy had
stood up by then and was one hundred percent
mountain man. Donna laughed at Sally as she
introduced her to Teddy and Toby. "How did you
ever get here Teddy?" asked Sally. "Walked all
but about a hundred miles," said Teddy. "Could
you ladies tell me how to get to the Evans Ranch?
I'll be getting on my way." He continued. "You
will do nothing of the kind young man. You will
stay right here until someone comes after you
or takes you to the ranch. How long has it been
since you have eaten?" asked Donna in her no nonsense tone of voice. "Couple of days since I
had anything but I can walk a little further
maam," said Teddy. "I'll bet you could but
your not going to. Sally heat up the grill and
throw on some bacon, eggs, and hashbrowns. I'll
stir up some pancake batter and we will feed
this Pioneer," said Donna as she hurriedly set
to work. "But I Don't have any money to pay
with," insisted Teddy. "Don't worry about money
Teddy, this is on the house. Anyone that walks
over a thousand miles to eat in my diner eats
for free," Donna laughed. "You stay right there
by the fire or go ahead and clean up in the bathroom while we get your breakfast Teddy." she
continued. "You could fix several meals while
I was cleaning up, I would imagine," said Teddy
as he headed for the restroom. "I haven't really
had good bath for what seems like forever," he
added as he turned on the light in the small room.
He stood and stared at the image looking back
at him in the mirror. He couldn't believe the
sight. His hair was down past his shoulders,
either suntan or dirt had made his face absolutely
brown and he had never gotten a good look at

92.

himself in buckskins. The smell of food drifting
from the kitchen shortened his clean up time
considerable. He didn't realize how hungry he
was until the smell of bacon frying hit his
nostrils. Sally and Donna just stared as he
entered the dining room. They had never seen
anything like Teddy before. Toby hadn't been
forgotten either . Donna had put about two
pounds of hamburger on to fry for the faithful
dog.

As they served Teddy his huge breakfast,
Danna said, "I'll call out to Joe and Nancy right
now. I know the phone lines are down to the
ranch yet after the storm. By the way where
were you during the storm Teddy?" In between
bites, he said, "We sat it out in a hole in
the ground covered with tree branches thanks
to Toby., If it hadn't been for him I would
have died out there." Donna was shaking her
head as she cranked the old phone two shorts
and two longs for Joe and Nancy's. Joe was
holding Andy and Nancy was nursing Annie when
the phone rang. At the same time the phone rang
Ann came to the door. She was on an early errand
to town for vaccine to treat some sick fall
calves. Joe answered the phone. "This is Donna,"
came the voice over the phone. "Have I ever
got a surprise for your sister, Could you get
her a message?" continued Donna. "Hold on Donna
she's right here. You give her the message."
replied Joe as he handed the receiver to Ann.
"Hello," said Ann. "Hi, say I have a young man
in here eatingbreakfast that says his name is
Teddy Springer," said Donna. Ann screamed
"Teddy!" She dropped the receiver and tore out
the door screaming, "I got to get to town.
Teddy's there." The twins were screaming now
with the sudden outburst from their Aunt. Joe
picked up the receiver and said, "Hello, hello,"
Donna knowing Ann the way she did had removed
the receiver far from her ear anticipating the
93.

scream. When she heard Joe's voice she said,
"I take it she got the message Joe," "I guess
she did," laughed Joe. "She will probably blow
Hank's old pickup up getting to town. Teddy
really made it then?" he asked. "He sure did
and is eating a huge breakfast," said Donna.
"Well you better hang up and prepare yourself
or my sisters entrance," said Joe as he hung
up. The twins had finally settled down and Nancy
said, "Boy, how many more surprises can we stand?"
"As long as they turn out like the last two we
can handle thenm," said her husband.

Ann was pushing the old ranch pickup for
all it was worth. Andy had told her to take
the tire chains off when whe reached the good
road but there was not time for that. One cross
bar had broken with the high speed and was
clanking loudly every time it came around. Ann
 didn't even hear it. She roared down main
street, slammed on the brakes in front of the
diner and never even parked or shut off the
engine. She was lucky to even get it out of
gear. Two jumps and she was hugging the daylights
out of Teddy. Toby was growling as he thought
she was hurting his master. "Look at you Teddy.
What happened to the cute little eight year old
boy that wanted to marry me?" Ann shouted.
"Well I'm thirteen now and just walked about
fourteen hundred miles, so guess it changed me
a bit, but I would still marry you if you weren't
already married," answered Teddy. Everyone roared
with laughter. Jake Phillips stuck his head
in the door and said, "Ann is it all right if
I park this pickup, shut off the engine, and
close the door?" "Sure after you meet Teddy
 Springer and Toby," said Ann. "Well I'll be,"
said Jake as he shook Teddy's hand. "We better
get a picture of this famous mountain man before
I take him to the ranch and convert him into
a cowboy," said Ann. I already thought of that

and called Hadly Farmer to bring in her camera.
She will want a picture and an interview for
the Pottsville examiner," replied Donna. About
that time, Hadly entered the cafe and was introduced to Teddy and Toby and started taking pictures. Teddy was speechless. He hadn't antici-
pated anything like this. After the pictures
were taken and Teddy was introduced to half the
town of Milligan, Ann said, "We better get the
vaccine and get to the ranch. Andy will be
shocked beyond belief." As she, Teddy, and Toby
left the diner Jake came driving up in her pickup.
"Heard you had a crossbar broken when I went
to park your pickup so I took her down to the
station and fixed it,"he said as he stepped out.
"What do I owe you?" asked Ann. "Forget it,"
said Jake as he entered the diner for his delayed
breakfast. Ann stopped just long enough to get
the vaccine and they headed for the ranch.

"Is everyone always this nice around here?"
Teddy asked. "Everyone I know is," replied Ann.
"You know, you worried your parents something
terrible don't you?" she said. "Yes and I'm
sorry about that but just didn't know what else
to do," said Teddy. "Well they have forgiven
you and have straightened out their lives since
you left. I am supposed to tell you that they
love you and are sorry for what they put you
through," said Ann. Tears welled up in Teddy's
eyes. "I love them too but don't know if I can
move back to Baltimore after living the free
life these last months," he answered. "Well
you won't have to go back. Your folks and I
have already worked that out, but you won't be
absolutely free either. You will have to finish
school and work on the ranch to earn your keep,"
said Ann. "No kidding!" exclaimed Teddy as he
hugged his dog. "You hear that Toby, we can
stay in Nebraska," he added.

They arrived at Joe and Nancy's and Ann
took Teddy and Toby in to introduce them. Joe
and Nancy were amazed at the sight of the boy.
They showed him Andy and Annie and he was faci-
nated. "They are so small Mrs. Jorden," he said.
"Call me Nancy," she replied. "They were just
born three days ago during the blizzard," she
added.

By now Ann was ready to head for the ranch.
Her and Em had been taking turns staying with
Nancy during the day while Joe was working.
It was Em's turn to come to help out and she
would need a ride in the pickup. "I'll bring
Em back as soon as I introduce Teddy and Toby
to her, Hank, and Andy," she called as her, Teddy
and Toby climbed into the pickup. Teddy asked
questions about the ranch as fast as Ann could
answer them. Finally she said, "I imagine you
have a few stories to tell about the last few
months don't you?" "Well, it has been quite
an adventure," replied Teddy. "Who's Becky you
left back home? Ever since we decided you were
headed this way hou have received a letter a week
from her," said Ann with a merry twinkle in her
eye. Teddy was embarrassed but his dark tan
covered the red that creeped up his cheeks.
"A friend of mine from Baltimore," he replied.
"Sounds like a girlfriend to me," laughed Ann
as they pulled into the ranch yard.

Hank and Andy were crossing the ranch yard
as they drove up. Ann and Teddy stepped out
of the pickup as the two men stared at Teddy.
"What in sam hill have you brought home with you
Ann?" asked Hank. "I would like to introduce
you to Teddy Springer and Toby," replied Ann.
Andy took it in his usual quiet manner but was
visibly surprised. Hank on the other hand was
his usual self also. "Well I'll be, are you
telling me this is the feller that harassed those
poor bank robbers in the Illinois hills?"

exclaimed Hank. "One and the same," said Ann.
"Well let me shake your hand young man. That
was about the most innovative thing I have ever
heard of," said Hank as he shook hands with Teddy.
"Has everybody in the country heard about that?"
asked Teddy. "You bet, it made national news
twice. Once when they caught the men and again
when they found the money," replied Hank. "They
did find the money then. I didn't know if my
map was good enough or if anybody would even
believe it," said Teddy. "You bet it was good
enough, good enough to earn you a thousand dollar
reward," added Hank. It was Teddy's turn to
be surprised now. Ann hadn't even had time to
tell him about the reward yet. "Maybe I could
use some of the money to buy me a horse and saddle
and I need some clothes if I'm going to help
on the ranch," said Teddy. "You don't need to
buy a horse or saddle around this ranch son.
We have enough for everyone," spouted Hank.

By this time, Ace had discovered Toby who
had saw the bigger dog and remained in the pickup.
Ace was growling at Toby and going to protect
his territory. "Ace you behave. That's a famous
dog in that pickup and he's going to live here.
He might not know anything about cows but he
catches bank robbers and has walked half way
across the United States. Call your dog out
her Teddy and introduce him," said Hank. Teddy
called Toby out while Hank held onto Ace. They
sniffed noses and Ace kept growling. Toby growled
some too but Teddy quieted him. Ace was more
adamant, as it was his ranch to protect. Hank
finally got him to behave just as Em emerged
from the house with her arms full of supplies
to go to Nancy's. She had a half-made afghan
that she was making for the twins. "Em I want
to introduce you to the famous Teddy Springer
and his faithful companion," exclaimed Hank.
"Well land sakes where in the world did you find
him Ann?" asked Em as she shook Teddy's hand

almost dropping her supplies. "Donna found him
sleeping in the kitchen of the diner," replied
Ann. "I sure didn't mean to break into Donna's
diner but the door was loose and I was nearly
froze," said Teddy. "Donna wouldn't care anyway.
She gives food away half the time. I don't even
know how she makes any money," said Hank. Finally
Andy spoke up. "Welcome to the Evans ranch Teddy.
I suppose Ann told you that your folks have agreed
 to let you stay here for a time and see how
you like it." "Yes she did and I am grateful
for that. After living outdoors and coming across
the mountains I don't think I could live in the
city again," said Teddy. "Can I take Teddy back
into town after I drop Em off at Joe's? We need
to go to the central office and try to get a
call through to his folks. We also need to go
to see Ted Barnes about some clothes for Teddy,"
said Ann. Teddy interupted, "Oh I have no money
yet to buy clothes Ann. I'll have to wait until
I can either work or get some of the reward money
to buy clothes." "Ted Barnes will charge the
clothes," spoke up Hank. "Besides money don't
mean much out here. When you need something
bad, people tend to look out for you," he added.
Em spoke up, "We better get going so Joe can
come back over to work." Teddy and Toby jumped
in the back of the pickup as Ann and Em crawled
in. Teddy spotted his backpack and finally remembered the letters Randy had sent with him. "Wait
Ann," he called. "I have something here for
Andy," he added as he dug through his pack.
He retrieved the two letters and handed one to
Andy. It was wrinkled and soiled from the long
trip. "Sorry about the condition of the letter
Andy," said Teddy as he handed it to him. Andy
looked puzzled as he took the envelope. "Who's
it from?" he asked. "Randy Silverfox," replied
Teddy. "He said you and him were prisoners in
the war together. I met him in the Appalachian
Mountains and he is the only reason I survived
98.

the long trip out here. "Well I'll be," said
Andy as Ann started the engine and drove off.
"It's a small world I guess," said Andy as he
and Hank watched the pickup drive off. "Open
it and see what he wrote," insisted Hank. Andy
opened the letter and read out loud. "Dear Andy,
Hope this letter finds you all well. Seems in
a roundabout way our paths cross again. I am
sending this with a young runaway that I have
learned to like very much. He has been a fine
student of nature and survival and I am sure
he will reach your ranch. I have tried to outfit
him and prepare him for everything he might
encounter but can't foresee everything. When
he reaches your place, please send me a note
telling me of his safe arrival. You can send
it to my brother Eddie and he will get it to
me as I live in seclusion in the mountains.
Seems like the war left some scars I am having
trouble dealing with. By the way, when he gets
there tell him the twenty-two rifle is his.
He wouldn't have taken it because he had no money
to pay for it, so I told him I was just loaning
it to him, and he could return it later. Hopefully, we can meet again someday. I an including
Eddie's address at the bottom of the page. A
fellow P.O.E., Randy Silverfox."

The old rancher and his son stood for a
long time after Andy finished reading. Finally
Hank said,"Makes a fellow pretty sure that a
supreme being has a hand in this thing called
life, don't it son?" "It sure does Dad, it sure
does," said Andy as his eyes clouded over for
an instant with almost undecernable tears.

Ann guided the pickup into Joe and Nancy's
yard. Teddy jumped out with Joe's letter in
his hand. Joe holding Annie in his arms met
them at the door. "Thought maybe you forgot
me this morning," he said. "Well I had to
99.

introduce Teddy to everyone and you know Hank.
I could hardly get away," said Ann as they entered
the house. Teddy approached Joe with the rumpled
letter in his hand. "Joe I forgot to give you
this before. It's a letter from a man that says
you and some other men saved his life in Europe.
He taught me everything he could about surviving
in the mountains and living with nature and that's
the only reason I made it out here," said Teddy.
Joe had a blank look on his face. How could
Teddy have met up with one of the former P.O.W.s?
He handed little Annie to Ann and took the letter.
While he was opening it, Nancy said, "Read it
to all of us Joe."

Joe started, "Dear Joe, I look upon this
as an opportunity to try to repay you to some
extent for what you and your men did for me in
Europe. This young man says he is traveling to
Nebraska to see if he can live with your sister.
He is a fast learner and willing to
work hard. I'm sure he will earn his way no
matter what he does. I am still indebted to
you for the courage you and your troop showed
when you rescued us. I hope in some small way
helping Teddy has repaid you a bit for what you
did for me. I hope to visit you folks out there
one of these days.. Forever in your debt, Randy
Silverfox. Randy Silverfox," repeated Joe as
he thought back to the day Danny Tibbs was writing
down all of the prisoners names. "He had to
be one of the Indian guides that was in the P.O.W.
camp. How did you run into him Teddy?" asked
Joe. "He found me half starved and with my clothes
and shoes wore out while I was passing through
the mountains," said Teddy. "He lives up there
alone. Kind of hiding from the real world he
told me," he continued. "Well it's a small world
that we live in," said Joe. "I sure hope I get
to meet Randy again," he added. "I have to get
his gun back to him some way," said Teddy. "He

loaned it to me and it's a good thing he did
or I never would have made it here," he explained.

"Well I better get to the ranch," said Joe.
"Can we borrow you car Joe? I need to take Teddy
into town to call his parents, get clothes, and
other things," said Ann. "Yes go ahead. I'm
sure you can make it into town alright with the
car but you better not try to get back over to
the ranch with it," said Joe as he pulled on
his coat and headed for the pickup. "Do you
need any supplies from town Nancy?" asked Ann
as she helped her sister-in-law lay the twins
on the bed. Nancy gave her a short list of things
they needed from town and her and Teddy prepared
to leave. "You feeling alright Nancy?" asked
Em before Ann and Teddy went out the door. "I
feel fine," replied Nancy. "Well I'll worry
about you until the weather clears up and we
can get you, Annie and little Andy over for a
checkup," said Em. "Nothing to worry about
with a midwife and nurse like you around," called
Ann as they went out the door. "Will it be o.k.
if Toby rides in Joe's car?" asked Teddy as he
walked beside them. "Sure," replied Ann. "It
will take awhile for him to get used to staying
without me after all these months together,"
said Teddy.

They crawled into the car and headed into
Milligan. "Think we will be able to reach my
folks?" asked Teddy as they bumped along. "I
hope so," replied Ann. After a short silence
Teddy said, "Sure hope they aren't too mad at
me." Ann laughed cheerfully and replied, "They
will be so glad to hear your voice that they
won't even think of being mad."

Finally they pulled into town and stopped
in front of the telephone office. Ann rapped
on the door and opened it when a voice shouted,

"It ain't locked." They entered to find Elizabeth
Hanks setting at the switchboard. "Sit down
a spell, I'm trying to connect Larry with one
of his lumber suppliers. It will be just a
minute." Elizabeth knew everyone within two
hundred miles it seemed and many more further
away than that. Finally she got the call through
and turned to Ann and Teddy. "Well I'll bet
this must be the pioneer lad that the whole town
is talking about," she said, as she looked Teddy
up and down. He was embarrassed by the attention
he was getting. "Where is that famous dog of
yours son?" she asked next. "He's out front,"
replied Teddy. "In this weather," said Liz as
everyone called her. She immediately went to
the door and let Toby in beside Teddy. "Now
what can I do for you folks?" asked Liz. Ann
explained the situation and LIz wrote down Teddy's
old home phone number as he repeated it from
memory. "I don't have money to pay for a call,"
he said. "Don't you worry son, we have to get
word to your folks that you are here. Money
is no object in an important matter like this,"
said Liz as she listened in to see if Larry was
done talking. The long distance line was clear
so she got out her directory and looked up
Baltimore and started calling for connections.
Teddy was pretty nervous as they waited for Liz
to get through to his folks.

After some time Pat Springer's phone rang
in Baltimore. "Hello," said Pat, not suspecting
the significance of the call. "Hi is this Pat
Springer," said Liz. "Yes," replied Pat. "I
have a fellow here that wants to talk to you.
Hold on a second," said Liz. Ann pushed Teddy
to the chair beside Liz. Liz placed the head
set on Teddy. "Talk to your Mother," whispered
Ann. "Hello Mom," said Teddy weakly. "Louder,"
said Liz. "Hello Mom!" said Teddy again. Pat
was almost speechless for a minute. "Teddy!"
she finally exclaimed. "Is that you Teddy?"
102.

she asked. "Yes Mom it's me. I"m sorry for
what I did but I couldn't stand to see you and
Dad like you were. I love you Mom," said Teddy
as tears came to his eyes. "Oh Teddy I love
you too and I'm sorry for what we put you through.
Dad and I have staightened out our lives though
and we both feel better than we have for a long
time," said Pat. "I'm really glad to hear that.
Will I be able to talk to Dad?" asked Teddy.
"Yes you will son but your operator friend will
have to call his office. I'll get you the number
for her. Are you all right Teddy and is Toby
with you?" asked Pat excitedly. "Yes Mom I'm
fine and Toby is right here with me. He saved
my life twice but I can't tell you all that on
the phone it would cost a fortune," replied Teddy.
"We will pay the phone bill Teddy. Put the operator back on and I will give her Mr. Goodwin's
number so you can talk directly to your Dad.
We have prayed together every night and morning
for your safety. Goodbye for now Teddy. Write
us a long letter son. Love you," said Pat.
"I love you too Mom bye," replied Teddy. He
handed the headset to Liz and smiled broadly
at Ann as she put her arm around his shoulders.
"Went pretty well didn't it?" she asked. "Yes
mom sounds great. I hope dad is that easy to
talk to," said Teddy. It was awhile again before
the phone rang in Mr. Goodwins office. "Hello,"
said Mr. Goodwin. "This is Goodwin Design, Ed
Goodwin speaking," He continued. "Mr. Goodwin
I have an important call for Arlo Springer,"
said Liz. "May I ask who is calling as Mr.
Springer is in a consultation meeting with two
clients," said Mr. Goodwin. "Just tell him
it's a call he has been waiting for about nine
months," replied Liz. "Teddy!" exclaimed Ed
Goodwin. "Yes," said Liz. "I'll have him in
a jiffy." said Mr. Goodwin and he rushed into
the next room. "Pardon me gentlemen, but Mr.
Springer has a very important phone call in my

office," said Mr. Goodwin as he entered the room.
"Can I call them back?" asked Arlo. "No you
can't. Now go take the call," said Ed in a matter
of fact tone. Arlo went into the office and
Mr Goodwin explained the situation to the
clients. "Hello," said Arlo into the phone.
"Hello, is this Arlo Springer?" asked Liz. "Yes
it is," he replied. "Hold the line while I put
this young man on," answered Liz. Arlo's heart
raced when she said young man. "Dad," said Teddy.
"Ted is that you?" shouted Arlo almost overcome
with excitement. "Yes Dad, it's me and I'm sorry
I couldn't contact you sooner," replied Teddy.
"It was more my fault than yours son. It's so
great to hear your voice. Your mother and I
have prayed every day for your safety. Does
your mom know you are alright?" asked Arlo.
"Yes, I just talked to her. Dad she sounded
great," said Teddy. "She is great. I am too.
What you did made us take a long hard look at
ourselves and we didn't like what we saw. We
have that all straightened out now though and
we will want to see you as soon as we can come
to Nebraska and visit the ranch," said Arlo.
"You would come out here Dad?" asked Teddy.
"Yes we would son, we might try to make it a
Christmas trip since it's not far off. We want
to see where you're living and meet the people
out there," replied Arlo. "That would be great
Dad. It would be my best Christmas ever," said
Teddy. "Is Toby o.k.?" asked Arlo. "Yes he's
fine," said Teddy. "I'll write you and Mom a
long letter and send it right away Dad. I love
you," added Teddy. "I love you too son. Take
care of yourself. I better get home to mom now.
Goodbye," said Arlo. "Goodbye Dad," replied
Teddy and he handed the headset to Liz. Tears
were running down both cheeks now as Ann hugged
him.

Arlo rushed back into the adjoining room,
"That was Teddy," he almost shouted to a smiling
Mr. Goodwin. "Yes I know Arlo. I have explained
everything to Hank and Orville and we have set
a new meeting time for tomorrow at three p.m.
You get home to Pat and here's ten dollars.
Take her out to dinner," said Ed Goodwin as he
shoved a ten-dollar bill into Arlo's hand. "But
that's way too much money for supper Mr. Goodwin,"
said Arlo as his boss was handing him his coat
and hat. "Well for the balance of the ten I'll
expect a full story of how that young man made
it fourteen hundred miles on his own," said Ed
as he pushed Arlo out the door. "He's going
to write right away. I'll bring the letter
to the office," said Arlo as he rushed down the
front steps to his car. He broke the speed limit
as he roared his car through the
Baltimore streets. Pat was watching out the
front door when the car pulled up and ran down
the walk to meet Arlo. They said nothing as they
embraced for a long time both crying freely.
Then they knelt right there in the yard and
thanked God for Teddy's safety. Finally Pat
said, "We have to call Becky and tell her."
They rushed into the house and rang Becky's phone.
Her mother answered and listened as Pat told
about Teddy. "Becky's not here right now but
I will tell her as soon as she returns. She
will be delighted," said her mother. Pat hung
up the phone and hugged Arlo again. "Can you
believe it's finally over?" she asked. "No I
can't," he replied. They talked of the plans
to go out and see Teddy at Christmas. Finally
Arlo remembered the ten dollars and told Pat
he was supposed to take her to dinner. "I'll
change and be ready in a second," said Pat as
she rushed from the room.

Meanwhile back in Milligan, Ann and Teddy
were in Ted Barnes' general store. "So you need

clothes to convert this mountain man into a cowboy, is that right Ann?" asked Ted as he smiled
with a twinkle in his eyes." "That's right,"
replied Ann as she laughed at Teddy"s
embarrassment.

Chapter 13

THE GREAT CONVERSION

Ann and Ted Barnes began showing Teddy the
clothes he would need to live and work on the
Evans ranch. Ann said, "We will just get you
everyday clothes now. You won't be starting
to school until after Christmas so we won't worry
about school clothes until then." Two pair of
overalls, two long sleeved blue denium shirts,
several pair of socks and long johns were piled
on the counter. "This stuff will cost a fortune,"
said Teddy. "Well not a fortune but probably
most of your first months pay," said Ann. "Oh
I couldn't ask you folks to pay me if I am living
there," replied Teddy. "Don't worry Teddy Hank,
Andy, and Joe will expect much more than enough
work out of you than your board and room will
be worth," said Ann. "I have known Hank Evans
for forty years, young man, and if you keep up
with him you will earn these new duds," said
Ted Barnes. "Now get over here and try on some
new boots," Ted continued. Teddy tried on new
boots until Ann and Ted were sure they fit.
"Sure do feel tight after wearing moccasins all
those miles," said Teddy. After they fitted
him with a coat, gloves, and a courdaroy ear
flapper cap he was all set. Ted wrote down each
of the purchases on a ticket. "Do I need to
sign that ticket?" asked Teddy. "No Teddy out
here if your word isn't any good your name on
a piece of paper is worthless also. We will
seal this deal with a handshake son," said Ted
as he shook Teddy's hand. "Next stop the barber
shop," said Ann as they left the general store.
Pete the barber bowed low as Ann and Teddy entered.
"Is this our new local hero?" He asked as he
shook Teddy's hand. Teddy still couldn't get

over the big deal everyone was making of him.
"Yes, the last of the mountain men. Can't you
tell by the looks of the clothes and hair?"
laughed Ann. "Set up here young fella," said
Pete. "Tell me what you want done," he continued.
"Well I want my hair cut like Andy and Joe wear
theirs, but I don't have any money to pay for
it," said Teddy. "This one is on the house.
It's not every day I get to cut a celebraties
hair. Tell me how you foiled those big time
bank robbers while I trim you up," said Pete.
"How did you know about that?" asked Teddy.
"Thats all Hank Evans talked about for a month
after he heard it on the radio. He kept me up
with a running account of the whole thing,"
laughed Pete.

Before long Teddy looked like a new person.
He thankede Pete as he and Ann left the shop
and headed for home in Joe's car. Ann had picked
up the things Nancy wanted while Teddy was in
the barber chair. Toby kept looking at Teddy
and sniffing him as if he wasn't sure who he
was. "Is everyone that friendly and helpful
out here?" asked Teddy as they pulled into Joe's
yard. "Most people are. The ones that aren't
soon move on as everyone needs to help each other
out here to survive," replied Ann. "I like that,"
said Teddy with a big smile. "All those people
trust me and they don't even know me." He added.

It was well after dinner time as they carried
Nancy's supplies to the house. The twins were
taking their nap as they had just been fed and
changed. Nancy was laying down also. "I don't
suppose we dare go to the ranch with Joe's car,"
said Ann. "Oh no," replied Em. "Joe was here
for dinner and said in places the pickup was
about to get stuck. This nice weather and the
melting snow is really making the road a mess.

He said for you and Teddy to stay here until
he comes home and then we can take the pickup
home," continued Em. "Well Teddy we just as
well finish making you into a cowboy right here,"
said Ann. Teddy and Em helped her put water
on the cookstove to heat. Teddy refilled the
wood box while the water heated. Ann got the
tin bath tub from the spare room and sat it in
Joe and Nancy's bedroom as Nancy was resting
on the couch in the setting room. They carried
the water to the tub and Ann went to the car
and brought in some of Teddy's new clothes.
It sure felt funny to be taking a real bath
after almost eight months. Teddy scrubbed good
dried off quickly as it was chilly in the bedroom
and dressed in his new clothes. Ann whistled
as he came from the bedroom. "Boy look at that
Em! Sure is a good thing I'm already married
or I might take this young man up on his proposal,"
she laughed. "Who is this handsome young man?"
asked Nancy as she entered the room from the
setting room. "Meet Teddy Springer, ex-mountain
man," said Ann to her sister-in-law. "Boy what
a chonge," replied Nancy as little Annie started
to fuss and she went to check on her. "We will
have to keep him away from those young girls
in town," teased Em. "From the looks of the
pile of letters from a girl named Becky I don't
think they have a chance," teased Ann to Teddy's
embarrassment. Both babies were fussing now
so Ann ran to pick up little Andy. They both
needed clean diapers and were soon content to
lay and have aunt Ann fuss over them. "Land
sakes Ann you will spoil them like you have Andy,"
said Em. She still thanked God for the wife
he had sent to her son. Andy was sort of shy,
unlike his dad, and she had worried about him
ever finding an ideal mate. Especially one that
would be a ranchers wife. Well Ann filled that
bill as she was as out going as Andy was shy
andloved the ranch as much as old Hank himself.
109.

Before long they heard Joe pull up in the
ranch pickup. They were all beaming like little
kids, wanting to show off Teddy when Joe came
in. "Well I'll be. What have we here?" He
exclaimed as he looked Teddy over from top to
bottom. "Ann what have you done to our mountain
man?" He asked his sister. "Made him into a
cowboy," she replied. "Well you might have
made him look like a cowboy but I think we will
leave the actual job of making him into one to
the best teacher around, namely Hank," said Joe.
"Do you think he will teach me to ride and rope
Joe?" asked Teddy. "Ted by this time a year
from now Hank will have filled your head with
so much knowledge that you will be a full flegged
sandhill cowboy," replied Joe. "About half
of it will be nonsense to young man," said Em.
"Mind you don't believe everything that old joker
tells you or he will drive you nuts. I could
have shot him a dozen times the first few years
we were married until I finally realized that
most of his teasing was for his own entertainment
and the madder I got the better he liked it.
Now Ann was a different story. He has to lay
awake at night trying to get ahead of her. Does
my heart good to see the ornery old devil get
some of his own medicine," continued Em as she,
Ann, and Teddy prepared to leave. "See you all
tomorrow," said Joe as Ann kissed the twins goodbye and they headed for the pickup. Teddy and
Toby crawled into the back and Ann guided the
old pickup through the ruts to the ranch. "Don't
know why Hank don't buy a new pickup," said Em
as she nearly bounced to the top of the cab.
Ann looked back to see if Teddy and Toby were
still with them and replied. "You know he says
this old pickup has personality. I told him
it was kind of like his personality. Kind of
rusty and falling apart." "Hee, hee, hee,"
chuckled Em. "I think with you around Hank will

110.

live to be a hundred years old just trying to get one up on you," she added.

They pulled into the yard as Andy and Hank slogged across the sloppy yard. Teddy jumped from the back of the pickup right into the mud and water with his new boots. "Oh no we forgot overshoes," cried Ann as she looked at Teddy. "I have an extra pair stashed," said Hank. "Boy you sure done a job on this young feller Annie. Now for a few months of my expert teaching and him and I can run this ranch alone. We won't need the rest of these free-loaders around here," said the old man. "Hurmph!" snorted Em. "You wouldn't last three days around here without me to look after you," she added. "Oh I didn't mean you Emmy. We couldn't get along without you. I don't think mountain man here could cook as good as you," said Hank as he winked at Ann. "All you think about is eating," said Em. "Well I'm too old to think about anything else," chuckled the old man. "You hush Hank Evans," snapped Em. Andy just shook his head at his Mom and Dads antics and told Teddy how great he looked and how they were pleased to have him on the crew. Ace and Toby were still growling at each other but were slowly geting aquainted. "Come in for supper everyone," said Em. "I knew it would be a hectic day so I started a roast on the back side of the stove early this morning," she added. They soon sat down to a feast of roast with potatoes and carrots and the best gravy Teddy had ever eaten. After the morning meal at Donnas he had thought he would never be hungry again but he and Ann had completely missed dinner and he found himself putting away this delicious meal in fine fashion. After supper Teddy pitched right in clearing the table with Ann and Em. "Now son don't be spoiling these wimmen," said Hank. "Rule one of the cowboy code is keep your wimmen tough and mean," he

111.

continued. Teddy looked at Hank and smiled.
"I believe I'll be pretty good to Em after that
meal. If something should happen to you Hank
I might even ask her to marry me," said Teddy.
Everyone roared with laughter as Hank shook his
head and replied, "Oh no Lord how could you
send me another joker like Annie,"

After Andy and Ann went home Em moved Teddy
into Andy's old room. It was exciting for her
and Hank to have a youngster in the house again.
When his room was ready Teddy said to Hank and
Em, "I'm so thankful you folks are giving me
a chance to try my hand at ranching. I'll do
my best to be worthy of your faith."

After he shut the door to his bedroom Hank
said, "He talks a lot older than thirteen. I
guess that adventure made a man of him." "I
think your right," replied Em. Teddy lay for
a long time in the warm comfortable bed with
Toby beside him. What a day it had been. All
those hours of worrying weren't necessary at
all. These were some of the best people he had
ever met. His thoughts turned to his mom, dad,
and Becky as he drifted off to sleep.

The next day Teddy was up bright and early.
A hearty breakfast at Em's table and he and Hank
were ready to go to work. They met Andy in the
yord. The two dogs were still uneasy with each
other. Ace Didn't want any other dog taking
over his domain. Hank told him to behave himself
as he and Andy decided what they would do first.
The snow had melted off of all the high spots
on the meadow and winter pasture so they decided
to turn the spring calving cows back out to graze.
"Good thing we got this Indian summer after the
blizzard or we could run short of hay," said
Hank. Andy agreed as Ann walked up to the group.
"How was your first night on the ranch Teddy?"

she asked as Toby excitedly met her. She had
a way with animals and Toby had accepted her
immediately. Ace quickly jumped between her and
Toby. He didn't want Ann petting a strange dog.
She just laughed and scratched both dogs ears
at once. "I slept fine," replied Teddy," and
Em had a great breakfast," he added. "I'll bet
she did," said Ann. "I'm going to go stay with
Nancy and the twins today so I'll take the pickup
and let Joe come back over to work," she added
as she headed for the old beat up pickup. "Better
put gasoline in it Ann," called Andy. She waved
her answer as she cranked it up and headed to
the barrel by the shop. Andy went to check the
oil in his A John Deere and fuel it up to hay
cows. It had been a big job every day pitching
hay to all the livestock on the ranch. It would
be a big help to have at least half the cows back
out on winter pasture. Hank took Teddy to the
barn and showed him the horses all tied in their
stalls. "I'll feed grain Teddy while you go
into the hay loft and pitch hay down each
chute to the horses," said Hank. Teddy scrambled
up the ladder to the hay loft and started to pitch
hay down. The loft smelled sweet as they had
put their best clover hay up there for the horses.
After all the mangers were full he crawled down
and found Hank working on an old saddle. It had
a small seat and showed many years of wear. "Son
this here was Andy's first saddle. With a little
repair it will be usable again and it will be
yours to use as long as you work here," said Hank.
"Really," replied Teddy, his eyes wide with
surprise. "Wish I had a horse to use it on,"
he added. "Don't worry son we have plenty of
horses to use around here," said Hank. They worked
on the saddle a while until they heard the pickup
return to the yard. "Run out and tell Joe that
Andy went to load a stack of hay and if he wants
to load another stack on the other skidrack we
will feed

113.

with two outfits beings we have another driver,"
Hank told Teddy. Teddy rushed out to deliver
the message. In the meantime Andy pulled through
the yard with a stack loaded already. Hank came
to the barn door just as Teddy finished telling
Joe what he had been instructed. "You go with
Joe and load Teddy. I'll go drive for Andy while
he starts pitching," called Hank as he headed
for Andy's tractor. Joe and Teddy headed for
the shop. Joe showed him how to check the oil
in the old tractor. Then he showed him how to
drain the excess tractor fuel from the carburator
into a small can and dump it back into the fuel
tank. He then shut the drain valve at the bottom
of the carburator and turned the lever to gasoline
on the dash. He explained that the tractor was
made to run on tractor fuel which was a lower
grade than gasoline but it wouldn't start as
good on fuel so they started them on gasoline
and then switched them to fuel. Teddy listened
intently to all of Joe's instructions. He wouldn't
forget anything he told him. Next Joe showed
him the petcocks that released the compression
on the cylinders so the tractor would crank
easier. "When it starts these have to be closed,"
said Joe as he pulled the choke and started to
spin the fly wheel. Suddenly the old A popped
and nearly scared Teddy to death. Joe laughed
as he reched up and pushed the choke in. One
more turn of the flywheel and the ractor was
running with the petcocks hissing loudly. Joe
shut the one on the left side while Teddy run
and shut the other one. When Teddy returned
to the other side Joe showed him how to turn the
lever to fuel. "Don't forget to switch the
fuel lever Teddy. The gasoline tank only holds
about two gallon and you will run out right away
if you forget to switch it," said Joe over the
sound of the tractor.

They drove out to the stack yard and Teddy
114.

held the tongue of the skid rack up while Joe
backed up to it. When the hole in the hitch
ws lined up with the hole in the tongue Teddy
dropped in the pin and they headed off to load
a stack. Teddy never missed a move as he helped
Joe load. They pulled the stack through the
yard and over to the corral where the fall calvers
were held. Hank and Andy had opened the gate
and let them back out into the calving pasture.
It would give them more room and take a little
less hay. They would still need hay as the grass
was shorter there than in the winter pasture.
Teddy opened the correl gate and Joe eased the
big stack through. Teddy crawled back up on
the tractor beside Joe and he pulled the stack
out into the pasture. Joe gave Teddy instruction
on how to put the tractor in low gear and gave
him an idea of where to drive. "Wait until I
get on top of the stack and then take off." said
Joe as he crawled off the seat. Teddy's heart
was racing as he waited to drive the tractor.
Joe had a little trouble getting on top of the
stack but finally with some help from the pitchforks he made it and called to Teddy to take
off. Teddy pulled the clutch back and waited
until the clutch pully stopped. He then shifted
into low gear. He eased the clutch in and the
tractor started slowly across the pasture. He
couldn't believe he was driving a real tractor.
He had gotten a toy for Christmas one year but
this was far from a toy.

By noon the cows were all hayed and the
spring calvers were turned back out into the
meadow. They headed to the house for dinner.
"What will we do after lunch?" asked Teddy.
"Out here it's dinner, not lunch Teddy," said
Joe. "That's one of the first things I learned",
he added. "O.K. I won't forget," replied Teddy.
"You and I have a special job after dinner,"

said Hank. "We don't care what Joe and Andy
do," he added. They entered the house to the
smell of Em's delicious meal. "Hows the new
hired hand doing?" asked Em as they came in.
"Not too good, he just called your dinner lunch,"
said Hank. "Don't pay any attention to him,
you did a fine job this morning," said Andy.

After dinner Joe and Andy went to replace
a cable in one of the winches while Hank and
Teddy headed out in the pickup. Hank had made
Ace stay home but let Toby go in the front of
the pickup. Ace wasn't too upset as he probably
hoped Toby would never come back. They still
weren't getting along very well. "Do you think
the dogs will ever be friends Hank?" asked Teddy.
"Sure they will, just give them time," replied
Hank. "Where are we going?" asked Teddy. "Over
to a neighbors," was all Hank said as they bumped
along. They passed Joe's house and pulled out
onto the gravel road. "Better take off the
chains," said Hank as they pulled to a stop.
Once the chains were stored in the back they
headed south down the gravel road. "The first
thing a cowboy needs to do is learn to break
a horse to ride," said Hank. "Think you could
do that?" he asked Teddy. "Well I used to watch
Ann at the stables once in a while when she baby
sat me in Philidelphia," replied Teddy. "What
a gal that Ann is," said the old rancher. "She
amazes me more each day. Don't you tell her
I said that though. I wouldn't want her to think
I was getting soft," said Hank. "I won't tell
her," said Teddy as they drove into Will Shanks
ranch yard.

Will was just coming out of the house.
"What you doing loafing around the house this
time of the day?" asked Hank to the old man
that came hobbling up. Many years of wild rides
and terrible wrecks on the range had taken it's

116.

toll on Will. "Don't get smart with me you old
codger," said Will, with a broad smile and a
twinkle in his eye. "Meet Teddy Springer my
new hand. This here is Will Shank Teddy. One
of the meanest most dishonest horse traders in
Nebraska," said Hank as they met in the yard.
Teddy pulled off his glove and shook Will's hand.
"Is this the young feller that walked halfway
across the country?" asked Will completely
ignoring Hanks description of him. "Sure is
and I'm going to educate him in the cowboying
business," said Hank. "Why don't you come live
with me young man. I know more about cowboying
than Hank will ever know," said Will. "Cut
the B.S. Will and show us that horse flesh you
told me about the other day," said Hank. They
walked to the correl by the barn where five two
year old colts were eating hay. Teddy looked
at the colts through the fence as Toby stood
watching. The colts were eating and playing
at the same time. "What do you want for choice?"
asked Hank. "One hundred and twenty five dollars
and don't try to jew me either," replied Will.
"Thats an outragious price. Which one do you
want Teddy?" said Hank all in one breath. Teddy
jerked around and looked at Hank expecting to
see him laughing at his latest joke. The old
rancher was dead serious though. "You want me
to pick one out?" he asked in amazment. "You
bet if your going to break him to ride you better
pick him out," said Hank. Teddy didn't know
what to say. "They are all just barely halter
broke," said Will. "You will have to do it all,"
he added. Teddy didn't know what to do. He
looked them all over and had no idea which one
would be best. "I won't be able to pay for one,"
he finally said. "I'm paying for the colt. You
will have to earn him by breaking him to ride,"
said Hank. Finally Teddy pointed to a black with
three white socks and a blaze face. "I guess he
will be my choice," he said. "Good choice," said

Will. "He will be a dang good horse with proper breaking," He added.

Will took a rope and stepped into the correl. With a swift move that Teddy hardly saw he dropped a loop over the blacks head and he began to fight. Hank hurried in and helped Will snub the colt to a post. They put a halter on him and then with him tied with the halter rope Will fashioned what he called a war-bridle out of the lariet rope. He made the loop very small and slipped it over the colts lower jaw. Next he ran the rope over his head and back through the small loop. He tugged it tight and untied the halter rope. The colt tore around the correl until Will jerked on the war-bridle and it tightened up. As he tried to lead the colt he would brace all four feet and wouldn't come. A couple of jerks on the war-bridle and the colt would lunge ahead. Hank manuvered the pickup, which already had a stock rack on it, back up to a high spot made especially to load horses. Will slowly manuvered the colt up to the pickup and handed Hank the end of the lariet which he snubbed in the front of the pickup. Hank kept the rope tight while Will slipped past the colt. Will grabbed another rope and threw one end to Teddy. Next Will instructed Teddy to go around the colt and he and Will brought the rope up behind the colt's rear end. He fought and lunged as Hank took up slack, but before long was in the pickup. They tied him with the halter rope and pulled the war-bridle off of him. Hank handed Will his rope and said, "foxy sucker isn't he?" Teddy and Toby stared wide eyed at the colt while Hank wrote Will a check.

Finally they were on the road home. "Well what are you going to name him Teddy?" asked Hank. "Foxy, I guess," replied Teddy. "Well he certainly is that," laughed Hank. Ann came

rushing out of the house when they stopped at
Joe's to put on the chains. "Oh he's beautiful!"
She shouted as she rushed up. Teddy was all
smiles as Ann looked at the colt. "He's Teddy's,"
stated Hank. "He is," squealed Ann. "What will
you call him?" she asked. "Foxy," replied Teddy
as he helped Hank with the chains. Ann was
alreay on the side of the pickup petting Foxy
and talking to him. The colt shook but stood
wide eyed as Ann talked to him. Hank just shook
his head and winked at Teddy. When the chains
were on Ann said, "wait for me. I'll get my
stuff and go with you. Nancy will be all right
until Joe gets home." It was late afternoon
when they pulled into the yard. Andy and Joe
came from the shop where thy were building a
new gate out of some new two by sixes Hank had
bought. They looked Teddy's horse over and
finally helped get him out of the pickup. With
everyone helping they soon had him in the special
stall Hank had made in the horse barn years ago.
"Put some hay and oats in for him Teddy," said
Hank. "We will let him settle down and the
breaking will start tomorrow," he added. Teddy
fed Foxy and when he came from the barn Joe had
left for home. Andy and Ann had went to their
house. It was sundown when he entered the house
for supper. "Hear you got a new horse," said
Em. "I'll look at him tomorrow," she added.
After supper Teddy wrote a letter to his mom
and dad and one to Becky. When he hit the bed
there was no laying awake that night as he was
completely exhausted.

The following days were filled with hard
work. Feeding in the mornings and working with
Foxy in the afternoons made time fly by. Ann
took Teddy to town to meet Mrs. Petes who would
be his teacher. She was really nice and asked
Teddy if he would talk to the class someday about
his trip to Nebraska. "They will be able to

learn a lot from your experiences Teddy," she
said as he and Ann left.

Time flew by and before Teddy realized it,
it was December twentieth and the day before Arlo
and Pat Springer were supposed to arrive in
Pottsville on the train. Teddy was so excited
he could hardly sleep that night. Andy, Ann,
and Teddy would leave early the next day to pick
up his folks. He had a funny feeling in his
stomach as he lay in bed trying to sleep. Even
Toby was restless beside him. Finally he drifted
off to sleep dreaming of his folks, his horse,
and his new friends.

TEDDY'S BEST CHRISTMAS

The day dawned bright and sunny. Indian
summer had been good to the Sandhills. Most
ranchers depended more on winter pasture than
the Evans ranch did. Lots of the ranches didn't
have as good of hay meadows as Hank did and there-
fore didn't put up much hay. They usually just
fed cotton cake as a supplement to the frozen
hill grass. Some of them just mowed and raked
the hay into windrows and let the cattle eat
it, as needed. Heavy snows tended to cover the
windrows and make them hard to find.

The good weather had cut down on feeding
chores considerable so Andy and Ann would be
able to leave them to Joe and Hank while they
took Teddy to meet his folks.

Teddy was up early and had breakfast. He
and Toby rushed out to feed Foxy before they
left for Pottsville. Toby would have to stay
home. He and Ace had finally made friends and
could be seen running and playing whenever they
had a chance. The road between the ranch and
Joe and Nancy's was better so they could take
Hank's Hudsen car to town. It was several years
old but had very few miles on it, as the pickup
was the vehicle of choice around the ranch.
Andy, Ann, and Teddy waved goodbye to Em, Hank,
and Joe as they left the yard. Nancy had started
to stay alone with her babies since Joe and Ann
had finally managed to get her to the doctor
for a check-up about ten days ago. The doctor
had been amazed at the twins and how good everyone
was doing.

When they reached Nancy's house, Ann hopped

out and ran in to see if she needed any supplies
from town. She said everything was fine and
she didn't need anything so they were soon on
their way to Pottsville. "You excited?" asked
Ann as she watched Teddy fidget nervously. "You
bet," answered Teddy. "I love it out here but
do miss Mom and Dad," he added. "Don't you
miss Becky?" teased Ann as she winked at Andy.
Teddy had kept receiving letters from Becky
since he arrived in Nebraska. He blushed but
had to admit he missed Becky also. She had been
his best friend in Baltimore. They cruised along
in the Hudson as if they were floating on air
compared to the old pickup. After what seemed
like an eternity, they pulled into Pottsville.
It was about ten-thirty and the train wasn't
due to arrive for about forty minutes. Andy
picked up a few veterinary supplies for the ranch
that wasn't available in Milligan. Then they
drove to the John Deere dealer and bought parts
for the magneto on one of the A John Deere's.

As they left the implement dealers, they
heard the train whistle blow and knew it was
pulling in. Andy guided the car to the depot
just as the train came to a stop. Teddy felt
really funny in his stomach as people began to
step off of the coaches. Suddenly he saw his
Mom emerge from the coach and ran to meet her.
She hugged and hugged him as the tears ran down
her cheeks. When she finally let him go, he
shook his Dad's hand but Arlo picked him up and
gave him a hug also. "Man you must have gained
thirty or forty pounds," said Arlo as he let
him down. A young girl was standing back a bit
from Arlo and Pat Springer. In the excitement
no one had seen her face clearly. Finally after
Teddy had greeted his folks, she stepped up and
said, "Hi Teddy". Teddy spun around and was
face to face with Becky. "Becky!" he shouted
as he gave her a big hug, which immediately

embarrassed him. "I didn't know you were coming along," said Teddy. He was amazed at how she had changed. She was no longer just a girl she was really grown up. "Thought she was just a good friend," teased Ann as her eyes twinkled with mischief and she winked at Teddy's folks. This added to Teddy's embarrassment and made everyone laugh. "My folks said it would be cheaper to let me come along than to keep buying postage for all the letters I was writing," said Becky. Arlo, Pat, Ann, and Andy shook hands and introduced themselves. Teddy had never seen his parents look so good. It was a merry bunch that climbed into the car for the trip back to the ranch. It was early afternoon when they arrived at Milligan. "Can we stop for dinner at Donna's Diner?" asked Ann. "Sure can," said Andy as they pulled up to the curb. The entire trip had been a constant stream of questions for Teddy from Becky, Arlo, and Pat. Everyone was still amazed at the feat he had pulled off. Arlo said more than once that he wanted to meet Randy Silverfox and thank him personally for what he had done for Teddy.

They entered the diner just as Sally and Donna finished with noon clean up. "Well look who's here. My mountain man," said Donna as they entered. Ann introduced everyone and Donna said, "No one will ever know the surprise it gave me when I found Teddy and Toby sleeping in my kitchen that morning." "From the looks of the pictures we received, I think I would have been scared," said Pat. "We have a picture of you and Toby hanging in our classroom Teddy. Mrs. Carr put a sign under it saying, the last mountain man," said Becky. Teddy just grinned from ear to ear. He bet some of the boys in his class envied him to no end. "Have you folks had dinner?" asked Donna. "No we haven't," said Ann. "Well sit up and Sally and I will serve,"

123.

said Donna as she pushed two tables together
to make one big one. Sally and Donna brought
out a big platter of roast beef, potatoes, gravy,
and corn that was left from their dinner special.
Sally and Donna joined the others as they ate,
as they hadn't had dinner yet either. They spent
the better part of an hour visiting and eating
before Andy said, "We better head for the ranch.
It gets dark mighty early this time of the year."
Arlo pulled out his wallet. "I'll pick up the
tab," he said. "No charge for this," said Donna.
"You just saved Sally and I having to put all
these leftovers away," she added. "Oh but it
was delicious,. We really should pay," insisted
Arlo. "No if Donna says it is free she means
it. It's a standing joke around Milligan that
no one knows how she makes any money when she
gives her food away," said Ann. "It makes for
good customer relations," laughed Donna as everyone prepared to leave. They all thanked Donna
and Sally and went to the car.

Joe was home by the time they reached his
place. They stopped and although Joe had met
Arlo and Pat when they all lived in Philidelphia
he hardly remembered them. The twins were the
center of attention as usual and behaved very
well for the guests. "Better get to the ranch
now Em has been preparing a feast for supper,"
said Joe. "More food," said Arlo. "I'll have
to help pitch hay if they keep feeding us like
this for a week," he added. "You will never
go hungry around Mom's house," said Andy.

The sun was setting as they drove into the
ranch yard. Ace and Toby rushed out to meet
the car as it came to a stop. When they stepped
out, Em and Hank were on the front porch waiting
for them. Ann went through the introductions.
When she got to Becky, Hank said," "Taking a
big chance bringing a pretty young filly like
that out here. These cowboys are liable to hurt

one another fighting over her." Everyone laughed
as Becky's face turned red with embarrassment.
As they entered the house the big old table was
set for a feast and the smell was delicious.
As they finished eating, Arlo said, "Does your
phone work? I want to call Baltimore and quit
my job. It's obvious you people need me around
here to help get rid of all this food," Teddy
smiled at his dad's joke. He had never seen
him have a good time like this before. Things
sure were different. Ann, Pat, Becky, Teddy,
and Em soon had the table cleared off and dishes
done. They all visited for an hour after supper
with Hank taking center stage when he told them
how he had laughed when the bank robber story
came over the radio. "Couldn't get him to talk
about anything else for a week," scoffed Em to
everyone's delight.

Sleeping arrangements were worked out with
Becky going home with Ann and Andy. Arlo and
Pat would take Teddy's bed and he would sleep
on the couch in Hank and Em's sitting room.
Everyone finally said good night and headed for
bed. Teddy lay awake again for a long time.
He was so proud that his mom and dad had
straightened out their lives and boy was Becky
ever pretty. He drifted off to sleep with his
arm over the edge of the couch touching Toby.
Toby had become his security symbol on the long
trip out here and would be until he was no longer
with him anymore.

The days before Christmas flew by as they
were filled with activity. Teddy had to show
his folks and Becky every inch of the ranch that
they could see with the snow like it was. He
didn't neglect Foxy and Arlo and Pat were amazed
at what Teddy had learned about breaking a horse
to ride. He also amazed them with how grown
up he was. What they didn't realize was their

own problems had aged him considerably
faster than most kids. Well their drinking was
behind them now and neither Pat nor Arlo could
remember when they had felt this good. Toby even
warmed up to Arlo after some coaxing. It
was hard for the dog to forget the times Arlo
had kicked him and yelled at him when he was
drinking.

Teddy and Becky spent hours walking and
talking. The day before Christmas they walked
to the mailbox after the mail. "I love it out
here Ted," Becky said as they walked along.
"So do I," replied Teddy as he looked at Becky.
She sure is pretty he thought. "Could you ever
live out here when you grow up?" Teddy asked.
"Oh yes," replied Becky. "I would love to live
out here. I get tired of the noisy city and
haven't had this much fun ever," she added.

"I hope you can come back some summer and
stay awhile," said Teddy. "I'll start working
on my folks as soon as I get home," said Becky
excitedly. "Do you think I could get a job out
here?" she asked. "I'll ask Ann if she knows
of anything you could do while you were here,"
said Teddy. They reached the mailbox and Becky
retrieved the mail. "I'll carry that," said Teddy
as he reached for it. Before either he or Becky
knew what was happening they were in each
others's arms. Becky pulled him close and
kissed him on the lips. His face burned furiously.
He had never kissed a girl in his life. Becky
giggled nervously as she pulled away and holding
onto Teddy's hand started for the ranch house.
They walked in silence for quite a while.
Finally Teddy said, "I like you a lot Becky."
She just laughed and replied, "I know that you
dummy. I've liked you a lot for a long time."
"We better not walk in holding hands. Hank and
Ann tease enough without seeing that," said Teddy.

126.

"Boy that's for sure," said Becky as she let
Teddy's hand go and ran the rest of the way to
the ranch house. As they entered the kitchen,
Ann was helping Em finish setting dinner on the
table. "Boy it took you two long enough to get
the mail. We better send a chaperone with them
after this," said Ann. Teddy felt his face burning
again and Ann chuckled at him.

Tomorrow would be Christmas and the day after
that Arlo, Pat, and Becky would be leaving to
return home. Teddy had a funny feeling in his
stomach every time he thought of them leaving.
It had been a great few days with his folks and
Becky there. They spent the rest of the day
helping Em prepare for Christmas Eve supper.
Joe and Nancy brought the twins over by mid afternoon to everyones delight. Teddy, Arlo, Hank,
and Joe entertained them while the women prepared
for Em's traditional oyster soup supper. It was
up to Em's usual standard with enough food for
twice as many people as was there. No one stayed
long after the supper dishes were done, as tomorrow
would be a big day. Everyone would again gather
at Em's at her insistence for turkey dinner with
all the trimmings.

Christmas morning dawned bright and sunny.
As day light broke Hank, Arlo, Joe, Andy, and
Teddy were already heading out to cake the cows.
Arlo found he enjoyed seeing the cattle more than
he had imagined so he went along every morning
to feed. They had cut back on haying as the nice
weather had melted much of the snow on the meadows
and the cows were picking every day. The men
loaded the one hundred pound sacks of cotton seed
cake into the pickup. Two pounds of cake for
each cow is what they fed. Arlo was amazed as
Teddy helped load the sacks of cake. He found
himself struggling with them, as the bulky weight
was hard to handle. Hank, Ace, and Andy crawled

127.

in the cab while Joe, Arlo, Teddy, and Toby hopped
on top of the cake sacks. They drove to the
pasture where the fall calvers were. The calves
were frisky this cold winter morning and ran in
a big circle as the pickup pulled into the pasture.
Hank had told them to put an extra bag of cake
in for the fall calvers as he had noticed quite
a few calves had started to eat cake. Hank only
had to honk the horn a couple of times and cows
and calves were streaming in from all directions.
The men in the back opened sacks and dumped a
steady stream of cubes onto the dry grass as Hank
idled along slowly. "That's it here," called
Joe as they dumped the last bag. The old rancher
sped up and headed for the spring calver pasture.
After feeding them they stopped at the windmills
and cleaned the ice out of the tanks.

They finally headed for the ranch house.
Teddy and his dad went to feed the horses while
Joe and Andy went to pitch hay to the replacement
heifers. Hank bundled up the empty gunnysacks
and cleaned out the pickup. He also hung the
empty sacks from the rafters in the feed shed
to keep the mice from chewing holes in them.
They would come in handy for many other uses.
Many times in his life Hank had soaked gunnysacks
in a stock tank and used them to beat out prairie
fires.

All the men finished their particular tasks
about the same time. Hank, Arlo, and Teddy were
in the yard when Joe and Andy came from haying
the heifers. "Teddy run get some vaccine and
a vaccinating gun from the house. We have a calf
with foot rot," called Andy as they approached.
"If Arlo and Teddy help me doctor the calf, you
can head home to get Nan and the twins," Andy
said to Joe. "I'll help," said Arlo. With that
Joe headed for his car to bring his family to

128.

the ranch. Teddy returned with the vet supplies
and they headed out to doctor the calf.

With the chores finally done the men headed
to the house and entered to the smell of roasting
turkey, baking pies, and all the side dishes Em
could think of. About a half-hour later, Joe
returned with Nancy and twins. Becky raced to
the car to help with little Ann and Andy as she
had fallen in love with them the first time she
saw them. Aunt Ann was right behind her and the
race to the babies was a close one with Becky
only winning by a step. Ace and Toby ran around
the car parking furiously creating quite a scene.
Joe just sat behind the wheel smiling and shaking
his head. "Look at the race Nancy," Joe said
laughing. "I guess we don't have to worry about
the twins if something happens to us," he added.
Nancy just laughed and handed little Annie to
Becky and Andy to Aunt Ann. The two turned and
headed to the house with their prizes.

Before long, they were all gathered around
the big table. Hank asked the blessing in his
rough old way. "Lord bless this gathering and
these new friends we have made. Also bless these
two new babies that they might grow up to be good
sandhillers. Amen," said Hank in his usual blunt
manner. There was a murmur of amens around the
table and Ann thought she saw a small tear in
the old rancher's eyes as he ended his short
prayer.

The food was delicious and everyone over
ate. The men retired to the living room except
for Teddy. He helped the women clear the table
and scrape and stack the dishes to be washed later.

Finally they all gathered around the living
room and Becky and Teddy handed out the gifts.
129.

All the presents were modest and useful. Teddy
had made all of his gifts for his folks and friends.
He had made his mom and dad a birdhouse and bird-
feeder. He made Hank a new Bootjack with Andy's
help. He and Andy had made small sleds for the
twins although it would be sometime before they
could use them. Unknown to Becky he had managed
to buld her a pair of bookends just since he found
out she was with his folks. Teddy, Andy, and
Joe had built Em a picnic table and hid it in
the shop until now. After all the gifts were
opened, Joe, Andy, and Teddy carried the picnic
table out for Em to see. Arlo and Pat had brought
gifts from Baltimore. They had bought Teddy new
cowboy boots but he had grown so much since they
had seen him last that the boots wouldn't fit.
They would have to return them and send the larger
ones back by mail.

After showing Em her picnic table, they
returned to the house where the twins were the
center of attention. "When will they be able
to talk?" asked Becky. "It will be quite awhile,"
said Em. "I wonder what their first words will
be," said Becky. "Probably Mama or Dada," said
Ann. "I'm going to teach them to say Grandpa
since I don't have any grandkids of my own," said
Hank. Winking at Ann as he said it. Ann
immediately jumped up and went and sat on the
old rancher's lap. She kissed him on the slightly
balding head and said, "Think you can wait six
months Grandpa?" The room was suddenly quiet.
Andy's broad grin was the only hint that he already
knew. Suddenly Ann's words sunk in and the room
erupted with shouts. "Ann's going to have a baby,"
shouted Nancy. Hank, who was used to being
upstaged by his daughter-in-law by now, was
grinning broadly and hugging her. "Land sakes
girl you been in that condition three months and
riding horse and working like you do. you have
to take it easy," said Em. Everyone laughed,
130.

as they knew Em would have her eagle eye on Ann
from now on. "Well what more could a man ask
for at Christmas than the promise of a grandson,"
said Hank. "Who said anything about a grandson,"
said Ann. "It may be a girl you know," she added.
"Nope it will be a boy," stated Hank. Well the
battle was on with Hank insisting on a boy and
Ann saying she was sure it would be a girl just
for the sake of argument.

The day was slowly waning and Teddy could
feel that funny sensation in his stomach as he
remembered tomorrow would be departure day for
his folks and Becky. He felt like a little boy
again and almost wished he were returning with
them. He knew though that this was the life for
him and his folks were coming back next spring
for a visit. Hopefully Becky could talk her folks
into letting her come out all summer to work.
He had asked Ann about a job for Becky and she
had said she would ask Donna if she could use
her in the diner. He sure hoped that would work
out. Everyone was visiting when Becky whispered
to Teddy. "Let's go start the dishes for Em and
surprise her." They slipped out to the kitchen
and quietly started the dishes. Most all of the
dishes were done before Ann discovered them and
reported to everyone what they had done. "Well
I got two big presents," said Em as she looked
at her clean kitchen.

Everyone had a small lunch and it was time
for Nancy and Joe to take the twins home. Finally
Ann, Andy, and Becky went home also. Teddy and
Toby sat together and talked to Pat and Arlo after
Hank and Em had retired. "We are proud of you
Ted," said Arlo. "You have made a big difference
in our lives and we love you very much," he added.
Tears came to Teddy's eyes as he hugged his dad.
He had never heard him say he loved him when he

was still drinking. Pat had tears in her eyes
as she kissed him good night and they went to
bed. Teddy sat and petted Toby a long time before
laying down. Even then he didn't sleep for a
long time. His mind returned to Randy Silverfox
and the mountains. I wonder what Randy is doing
now he thought as he drifted off to sleep.

        The next morning they prepared to take Arlo,
Pat, and Becky to Pottsville to meet the train.
Hank, Em, and Joe were on hand as Andy, Ann, Teddy,
Arlo, Pat, and Becky loaded their luggage in the
Hudson and prepared to depart. "We will be looking
forward to your visit next spring," said Em as
they crawled into the car. Andy drove and Ann
sat beside him with Arlo next to the door. Teddy
sat in the back between his mother and Becky,
each one of them holding his hand. It was a pretty
quiet ride with the only conversation being Arlo
asking Andy things about ranching which he had
really became interested in. He knew nothing
about it and some of his questions were pretty
elementary with Teddy knowing the answers but
keeping quiet.

        They arrived in Pottsville just as the train
was taking on passengers. Teddy hugged his mom
and gave her a kiss, then he shook Arlo's hand
but his dad pulled him to him and hugged him
shortly. Becky hugged him and kissed him on the
cheek but he only felt a twinge of embarrassment.
They stood on the dock until the train pulled
out and then turned to go. As the Hudson purred
towards home all was quiet. Teddy sat where Arlo
had on the way down. Ann slipped her arm around
him and hugged him. "We are glad to have you
in our family," she said. "Your folks are great
people and I really like Becky," she added. "Mom
and Dad have really changed for the better and
Becky was sure grown up," said Teddy. "She's

132

a pretty girl," said Andy in one of his rare
comments. "She sure is," replied Teddy. "Sorry
you're not going home with them?" asked Ann.
"No," said Teddy. "I'll miss them but this is
home to me now and I'm going to do my best to
earn my way," he added. "Well first you have
to go back to school young man," said Ann. "Yes
I know," replied Teddy. "It seems like five years
ago that I went to school. It sure will be
different," he added. The road was smooth and
the constant purr of the engine soon put Teddy
to sleep as he hadn't slept well the night before.
As he nodded off to sleep, Ann cuddled close to
Andy, nodded towards Teddy and winked. Andy just
grinned and steered the Hudson towards home.

THE END